The Pot Thief who Studied the Woman at Otowi Crossing

J. Michael Orenduff

Spoiler Alert

We at Aakenbaaken & Kent know that some readers like to read the acknowledgements and other parts of a book before reading the story. Please refrain from doing so in this case as the ending is revealed in the Author's Postscript.

The Pot Thief who Studied the Woman at Otowi Crossing

aakenbaakeneditor@gmail.com

This book is a work of fiction. The characters are the product of the author's imagination. Any resemblance of the fictional characters to actual persons living or dead is entirely coincidental. Real persons mentioned in the story are depicted as accurately as possible based on written records. Almost all the places mentioned are real and described as the author remembers them.

Cover photograph of Mimbres pottery shard provided by Buddy Mays, former student at New Mexico State and an outstanding writer, photographer, and friend.

ISBN: 9781938436918

Praise for the Pot Thief series

"Orenduff successfully combines humor and homicide in his superb eighth Pot Thief whodunit"
Publisher's Weekly – starred review.

"An extraordinarily funny murder-mystery."
— *Baltimore Sun*

"Orenduff successfully captures the essence of New Mexico through humor, romance, and even a little philosophical musing. New Mexico's rich history, people, food, and landscape come alive on his pages." — Bill Richardson, 30th governor of New Mexico and former U.S. Ambassador to the UN.

"Orenduff's smartly funny series is filled with improbable situations, clever word play, and a good helping of fast-paced action. I love every twist and pun." — Best-selling author Anne Hillerman

"Light, amusing banter reminiscent of Lawrence Block's Bernie Rhodenbarr series." — *Denver Post*

"Orenduff perfectly captures the beauty of the New Mexican sunset, a good friend and a margarita. Throw in the occasional dead body, and it's pure enchantment." —*El Paso Times*

"Fun, amusing mysteries that allow readers to enter into the world of art and philosophy, science and murder. Buy a Pot Thief murder mystery, grab a margarita, and read up!" —*Mirage*, the University of New Mexico Alumni magazine.

Chapter 1

Susannah asked how I knew the guy on the ambulance gurney was dead.

"Simple," I said, "the sheet was pulled over his head."

"If you couldn't see the head, how do you know it was a guy?"

I shrugged. "I suppose it could have been a flat-chested woman wearing size 12 wingtips."

She ignored my sarcasm and said, "Maybe they were just trying to keep him warm."

"It's close to seventy," I pointed out. Even though it was early January, the sun hanging in the clear sky above the west mesa warmed the veranda at *Dos Hermanas Tortilleria*. The name is technically accurate because they do make and sell *tortillas*. But if the two sisters were to rename it based on what most of their customers buy, it would be *Dos Hermanas Cantina.*

The Albuquerque Visitors and Convention Authority likes to say we have "four mild seasons." What they neglect to add is that they often happen on the same day. My windshield had frost that morning, and now my jacket was hanging on the back of a chair on the veranda.

And what a jacket it is. Hand-sewn from horsehide by Sunny Seepu from one of the local pueblos, it has a secret pocket in the lower back with two layers of horsehide where I can carry a small artifact illegally unearthed. Comes in handy when a BLM agent meets me strolling out of public land shortly before dawn.

And why should I worry about that?

Because I'm a pot thief. I make my living digging up and selling ancient pottery. Yes, I know it's illegal. But it's not immoral. The women who made those pots don't want them to be buried forever. They want me to unearth their handiwork so that people can admire it. Which is why Sunny – who is descended from those ancient potters – made me the jacket. She knows I never dig in graves. It's not only wrong; it's pointless. The tradition of breaking pots as part of the burial ceremony means there's nothing valuable in there. What kind of ghoul robs a grave for mere shards?

"Maybe they were just shading his eyes from the sun," Susannah suggested. The woman has a quirky mind.

I told her Whit was standing next to the gurney.

She nodded knowingly and said, "And he's a homicide detective." Then she brightened and added, "Oh my god, Hubie. You've got the syndrome." She plopped her saltless margarita glass onto the table and stared at me wide-eyed. "I thought it was made up, but it's real. And you've got it. You've got the Jessica Fletcher Syndrome."

I love how Susannah's enthusiasm shows in her big brown eyes. But not when she's telling me I'm afflicted with something from the List of Terrible Diseases Named after People. Like Alzheimer, Asperger, or Lou Gehrig.

I rotated my glass to the part of the rim with salt and took a large sip. "What are the symptoms?"

"Dead bodies."

"God! It's fatal?"

"Of course it's fatal. Murder always is."

Now I was really confused. "Murder isn't a syndrome."

"The syndrome doesn't apply to the victims, Hubie; it applies to the people who find them."

"So this Jessica Fletcher woman was an expert at tracking down murder victims?"

"Not tracking them down. More like just always having murders happen everywhere she went."

I'd been headed to *Dos Hermanas* for the usual cocktail hour with Susannah when I saw the dead guy in the plaza just a block and a half from my shop in Old Town Albuquerque.

"So I've found a corpse or two. That doesn't qualify as 'always having murders everywhere I go'. I don't think I have the Jessica Fletcher syndrome."

When I heard myself say the last name, it sunk in. "Wait - now it makes sense. Jessica Fletcher must be Whit Fletcher's wife. He's a homicide detective, so naturally she'd have a lot of indirect connections with murder victims."

"I didn't know Whit had a wife – poor woman – or that her name is Jessica. But it's not the same person because the Jessica Fletcher the syndrome is named for is fictional."

"Syndromes aren't named after fictional persons."

She leaned back in her chair and stuck a fist in the air. "Rapunzel Syndrome," she said and raised her pointing finger. "Othello Syndrome." Her middle finger straightened. "Also, Peter Pan Syndrome. Mowgli Syn—"

"Okay, okay. I don't care who the syndrome is named after. I don't have it."

Even though I told her I didn't care who it was named after, she told me anyway. "Jessica Fletcher is a character in a television show called *Murder She Wrote*. It's been running forever."

Susannah is a big murder mystery fan.

I relaxed a bit. "Somehow I can't work up much interest in a fictional syndrome."

"Jessica Fletcher may be fictional, but her syndrome is real. And you *do* have it."

I opened my mouth, but she held up her palm and said, "Let's start with Guvelly."

"You also saw his corpse," I noted, "so

maybe you have the syndrome, too."

She shook her head. "I saw him only because you came and got me out of class to help you decide what to do with him. Which was a good thing since your idea was to dump him into the Rio Grande. Although I can't imagine why."

"That should have been obvious. It's the only river in Albuquerque."

"Geez. I wasn't wondering why the Rio Grande; I was wondering why dump him?"

"I was afraid if I told the police there was a dead guy in my shop, they might think I killed him."

"But we *did* call the police. Whit Fletcher in fact. And he helped you out."

"And made some money in the process."

"But at least justice was served."

We were both right. Whit is a good cop in the sense of going after the bad guys. But cash and valuables at a crime scene are apt to find their way into his wallet if they aren't evidence.

"So the next dead guy you encountered—"

"How about a second round?" I asked and signaled for our server, Angie.

Chapter 2

"What's your wife's first name?"

It was the next day and Whit Fletcher was staring at me from just outside the front door of my Old Town pottery shop, Spirits in Clay.

"Normally people say 'good morning' or 'hello'," he said.

"Sorry," I replied. "Good morning."

"How about 'come in'?" he asked as he shouldered past me.

I locked the door and followed him through the shop then the workshop and into what used to be my residence until I moved into Sharice's downtown loft.

Whit grabbed a mug from the shelf and poured himself a coffee. After taking a seat and a sip, he looked up and said, "Birdie."

"Birdie?"

"Right. Her real first name is Bertha, but she don't like it, so she goes by Birdie. Why you ask?"

He questions everything. Probably comes from being a cop. He thinks we're friends, and maybe we are. I don't dislike the guy. He's helped me out of a few jams even though he's also gotten me into some as well.

"I just wondered if her first name might be

Jessica."

He gave me a sour look. "That dame is a complete phony. Birdie watches the reruns every day. I explained to her a hunnerd times that the police work in that series is bogus, but she loves it." He took another sip then said, "Kinda warm in here." He stood up, removed his suit jacket and hung it on the back of the chair where it fit better than it did on him. Then he sat back down and said, "Have a seat, Hubert, so's I don't have to strain my neck looking up at you while I ask some questions. Not that you're much shorter sittin' down."

I ignored the jibe and lowered my five foot six inches into the chair across from him.

"Gimme an account of where you were yesterday from the time you woke up until I saw you at the gazebo."

"Why?"

"So's I don't have to run you downtown. The coffee at the police station's not as good as yours."

"Sharice woke me up in her condo about eight. We had one of our usual breakfasts, coffee and a *croissant aux amandes,* then she left for work."

"What the hell is a cwassoon amounder?"

"A French donut," I lied.

"Then I suppose the next thing you did is take Sharice's African wildcat and that mongrel of yours for a walk."

I nodded. The mongrel's name is Geronimo and he looks like a cross between a chow, a collie, and an anteater. The cat belongs to Sharice and is named Benz. My guess is his mother was named Mercedes. He's a Savannah cat, a breed created by crossing an African wild serval with a domestic cat. He looks like a smallish cheetah and fetches better than Geronimo. Unlike a domestic cat, Benz doesn't mind a collar and leash, so walking him is not a problem. Except for the stares I get.

Sharice, as you've probably surmised, is my girlfriend. Like Benz, her ancestors came from Africa. They were forcibly taken to Jamaica in the eighteenth century. Her father immigrated to Montreal a few years before Sharice was born, thus accounting for French being her first language, although she speaks English a lot better than Whit does.

Luckily for me, she moved to Albuquerque about five years ago. Her long limbs and petite hands captivated me the first time I saw her. The second time I saw her, those hands ended up in my mouth. It wasn't as erotic as it sounds – she was cleaning my teeth. She's a dental hygienist.

"Then what?" asked Whit.

"I took a shower, walked to Old Town, and spent the day in my workshop."

"Making forgeries."

"I prefer to call them copies."

"What you prefer to do is call 'em copies but sell 'em as genuine. Probably illegal, but I got more important things to worry about than you ripping off a few unsuspecting tourists."

"Like the guy on the gurney yesterday?"

He nodded.

"So why question me about my whereabouts?"

"Because you're a person of interest."

This conversation had an all-too-familiar ring. I put my mug down. I didn't need more stomach acid. Maybe Susannah was right about me having the Jessica Fletcher Syndrome.

"How can I be a suspect? All I did was stroll by?"

"You ain't a suspect. You're a person of interest."

Right, I thought. *Person of interest today. Suspect tomorrow.* "Why am I a person of interest?"

He handed me a folded piece of paper. I opened the fold and saw my name and the address of my shop. At first I thought it was engraved, but a closer look revealed is was written by someone with impeccable handwriting. I looked up at Whit.

He took the paper back and said, "The dead guy had this in the inside pocket of his suit jacket."

"Oh great. Now it has my prints on it."

"You know I'm a better cop than that. We already checked it for prints. People think you can't get prints from paper, but they're wrong. Sometimes we can. Unfortunately, this wasn't one of those times."

I was only half listening. The other half of my attention was focused on why the guy would have been carrying a paper with my name and address on it. The obvious explanation was he was coming to my shop.

Whit had the same idea. "You have any appointments yesterday?"

"Only with Susannah at five at *Dos Hermanas*. That's where I was headed when I saw the crowd in the Plaza near the gazebo."

"None of my business, Hubert, but it seems kinda suspicious you're still cavorting with that Inchaustigui girl given that you're shacked up with Sharice."

Inchaustigui is a Basque name and is pronounced exactly as spelled. Not that that helps. Her family owns a ranch nestled against the Gallinas Mountains. Ten miles north of the ranch is Willard, home to 214 people and the Willard Cantina & Café whose sign boasts "chili with attitude." There is no town to the south because of the mountains, but there is a wind farm along the ridge line. Its formal name is High Lonesome, which more or less sums up the area.

"We aren't *cavorting,* Whit. Never have cavorted. We're just friends."

"If you say so. What say you and me take a ride over to the morgue?"

Some of this morning's coffee and *croissant aux amandes* bubbled up into my throat. I ignored my acid tummy and took two sips of coffee to force it back down. I asked him why he wanted me to go to the morgue.

"See if you can identify the stiff," he answered.

"Can't you just fingerprint him?"

"We already done that. But we didn't get any matches when we ran them through the system."

"He didn't have any ID on him?"

"We think it was stolen."

"Why?"

"My theory is the murderer took it. Most murder victims are killed by people they know. Makes it harder for us to connect the killer to the victim if we don't know who the victim is."

"Or maybe the victim just lost his ID."

"Don't think so. His right back pocket was hanging out of his pants."

"Maybe that happened when he pulled out his handkerchief." I was stalling, hoping to think up some reason why I couldn't go to the morgue. Like extreme corpsephobia.

Whit shook his head. "Guy was like one of them faggy male models. Had manicured nails. Snappy dresser. Had on a suit from that expensive Italian guy Emeral Zenia. Cost more than I make in a month. And his shoes were from Salvador Fergaro, another expensive Italian brand."

"I'm surprised you know so much about men's fashion from Italy."

"I don't. Get my clothes at Suits Unlimited over on Menaul. Hunnerd and fifty a pop. But we inventory everything on murder victims – jewelry, clothes, even moles and warts. He didn't have neither of those last two. And a guy dresses like that don't leave a pocket turned out and flapping in the wind. On top of which, his handkerchief was in his lapel pocket, made of silk and neatly folded into three points. And here's something else that we found in a side pocket of his jacket." He handed me a pottery shard and asked if I recognized it.

"Sure, it's a piece from a Mimbres pot."

"I figured you'd know exactly what it is. Also figured maybe you sold it to the dead guy."

"I don't deal in shards," I replied. And to nudge the conversation in a different direction, I asked how the dead guy was killed.

"The white coat boys will decide the official cause of death, but I found a puncture wound in his back. Looked like someone jabbed him with a screwdriver."

I winced. "Sounds awful, but not like something that could kill you."

He stood up and put on his jacket. "You might change your mind when you see the wound."

"I don't want to see the wound."

"So that makes two things you're gonna see that you don't want to."

Chapter 3

I'd accompanied Whit to the morgue several years ago to identify a guy who turned out to be someone I had seen although I didn't know his name. I wasn't all that surprised to find him in the morgue. He had paid me twenty-five hundred dollars for appraising his collection of Anasazi pottery and then stolen the twenty-five hundred back. And done a lot worse to other people.

Even though I hated that experience, at least it served to steel me somewhat for this unwanted return. Whit positioned me to the left of one of the big drawers and told a guy who works in the morgue to stand on the other side. The morgue guy's eyes seemed unfocused. Maybe an asset for a morgue attendant. I briefly wondered what duties he had other than opening drawers, then realized I didn't want to know.

He slid the drawer out.

I closed my eyes and counted silently to five. I said to myself, *one quick glimpse*. Then I glanced down, saw the face, and immediately turned to Whit. "Sorry. Never saw him before."

"You didn't look long enough to know that, Hubert. You need to make sure, study his face."

"Already did. I'm a quick study."

"Okay," he challenged me, "gimme a description of him."

"Caucasian, medium complexion, brown hair professionally cut, good skin, no moles, scars or other distinguishing marks. Probably good looking when he was alive."

"Hmm. That's a good description. I guess you did look at him. Positive you never seen him before?"

"Positive."

My good description had been aided a bit. Whit had already told me the guy had no moles or warts. And noticing his hair color was easy because it was the same as mine, and the last haircut he'd had was so good that I noticed it because mine wasn't. Regarding ethnicity, you can't help noticing whether someone is black, white, Asian or whatever."

There was also something else I noticed, and it had me shaking – the dead guy looked familiar.

"Why you shaking, Hubert. Being next to a stiff make you nervous?"

"No. It's cold in here."

"Or maybe it's because you're withholding something from me."

"I'm not. I cannot identify him."

"Well, can't say I'm surprised," Whit said. "Probably heading to your place to buy one of them expensive pots. From the look of him, he could afford it." He looked at me in my well-worn jeans and clay-stained shirt and added, "And from the look of you, you could have used it."

"I've been throwing pots the last two days. I don't dress up for that. Or for trips to the morgue."

"You want to help us roll him over so's you can see the wound?"

"No way."

"What I figured. You're the sensitive artistic type."

"Making pottery doesn't make me an artist."

"If you say so. But digging it up makes you good money." He turned to the morgue attendant and said, "You grab the torso. I'll take the legs."

I looked up at the ceiling as they rolled him over.

"You can look now," said Whit.

I was staring at the ceiling. "Why do I have to see the wound?"

"Makes the ID process complete."

"You expect me to ID him by a wound?"

"I'll explain it later. But right now the poor guy's ass is exposed, so do us all a favor and look at the wound so we call roll him back over and put the sheet on him."

If my glance at him face-up was at the speed

of light, then my peek at his backside must have been at warp speed, whatever that is. The wound was as Whit had described it, a puncture about the diameter of a small screwdriver and surrounded by bruised tissue. I'll spare you a description of what was south of the wound.

After they rolled him back over and shut the drawer, Whit and I walked back to the lobby. The morgue guy stayed in the cold room. Whit signed out at the front desk, and we went outside and got in his car. "Reason I had you look at the wound is I figure you might help me out with this. You got one of them encyclopedia minds."

"I think the word you're looking for 'encyclopedic'."

"No. The word I'm looking for is 'explanation'. See, there was this tourist making a video of the Old Town Plaza, and the guy we just looked at happened to be where the tourist was aiming his phone. So being an honest citizen, he showed it to us. In fact, he even emailed it to us so's we'd have it on file. Ain't modern technology great?"

"Rarely."

"What the video shows is this guy walking towards your shop—"

"Wait! Yesterday you accused me of selling him a shard, and you knew all along he was headed *towards* my shop, not away from it."

"Just normal police procedure, Hubert. Rattle people; see what happens. So back to the video. Like I said, he's walking toward your shop. Then he shudders and falls face down. Now here's the weird part. There was no one close enough to have stabbed him. There was people around of course. There was one guy about six feet to his right and another guy about ten feet to his left, and a woman more or less directly behind him but even further back, say fifteen feet. But nobody close enough to drive a screwdriver into him."

"Maybe he was shot."

"Yeah, my first thought seeing the wound was small caliber, maybe a .22, but the pathologist said there was nothin' in there and no exit wound either."

I thought about it for a minute. "Maybe he'd been wounded the day before – fell and landed on a rake or something. He didn't know how bad the wound was, so he cleaned it up, rubbed on some disinfectant and slapped a bandage on it. Whatever punctured him nicked an artery but didn't completely pierce it. Then as he was moving around the next day, the weakened nicked wall of the artery suddenly broke, causing him to shudder then fall down and bleed to death."

"That ain't half bad. I'll run it up the flagpole and see if the lab guys salute it. You want me to take you back to Old Town or downtown."

"Downtown, please. I need to start dinner preparations before Sharice gets home."

"Ain't that sweet. You still planning on marrying her, Hubert?"

"If she'll ever say yes."

"What about her father?"

"I have no interest in marrying him."

"Always the jokester. I met the man, remember? He's a tough one."

Chapter 4

I walked Geronimo and Benz when I got to the condo.

Then I washed my hands, put two poblano peppers under the broiler, and chopped up some onions and *calabacitas*. I'd just removed the poblanos from the oven and peeled their skins (which was the point of blistering them) when Sharice arrived.

Her lingering hello kiss took my mind off the morgue.

"Is the Gruet cold?" she asked.

I pointed to the ice bucket on the coffee table and said, "The coupes are also on ice."

We moved to the loveseat and as I poured, she asked about my day.

"I went to the morgue."

"Poor baby. I know how squeamish you are."

"It wasn't so bad this time. In fact, what bothered me most wasn't seeing another dead guy – it was that he looked familiar."

"Lots of people look familiar."

"Yeah. But Susannah was kidding me yesterday about having the Jessica Fletcher Syndrome because I happened to walk by a dead guy on a gurney in the Plaza. There was an ambulance, and Whit Fletcher was there."

"And he made you go to the morgue today to identify the body."

"Right, which I couldn't because I'd never seen the guy before. But it just seems too Jessica Fletcher-like that he looked familiar."

She scooted closer to me and put her hand on my thigh. "You know you have a tendency to overanalyze. If you'd seen the guy when he was alive, you would've thought he looked familiar, but you wouldn't have worried about it. So just because he happened to be dead is no reason to worry about it."

She was right of course. I took a sip of the chilled New Mexico champagne and tried to relax. But she was laughing.

It was contagious and I started giggling. "What's so funny?"

"You want to forget about seeing a corpse, right?"

"I do."

"There was a time when I deliberately thought about cadavers to take my mind off something."

I shivered. "Really?"

She nodded. "I was in the throes of my bad reaction to docetaxel, the chemotherapy drug they gave me. I told you it sent me to the ER and then to the ICU for a week with diarrhea, vomiting, trouble breathing, throat swelling, and my lips and mouth covered with painful sores. At first I tried to concentrate on pleasant memories and picture fields of wildflowers in my mind, but it didn't work. I was sure I was going to die, which made me think of the cadavers I'd worked with."

"You worked with cadavers?"

"Of course. I was in dental school, remember?"

"You pulled dead people's teeth?"

"Root canals. And you know what we liked best about it?"

"There was something about it you *liked*?" I was finding this difficult to believe. Especially about the woman I love.

"Absolutely," she said with a mischievous grin. "The students liked it because cadavers don't bleed, don't feel pain, and don't complain. The only bad part is they also don't pay."

"So how did thinking about that help you forget the pain you were in?"

"Because gruesome things occupy the mind more aggressively than pleasant ones."

"Is there any evidence for that?"

She turned her palms up. "I'm not a shrink; I just clean teeth. Did the dead guy have good teeth?"

"I didn't see his teeth, but I imagine they were perfect. He probably had both a personal dentist and orthodontist."

"What makes you think so?"

"Whit told me the guy was wearing a suit from Emeral Zenia and shoes from Salvador Fergaro, which means he had loads of money."

She started laughing again. "Their names are Ermenegildo Zegna and Salvatore Ferragamo, but I can just imagine Whit butchering those names."

Sharice is an expert on *haute couture*. She dropped out of dental school after her mastectomy and took a job as a dental assistant/hygienist hoping to save enough money to pay for reconstructive surgery. She eventually abandoned that idea and used the savings to buy some designer dresses and make a down payment on her condo. Those dresses made her feel a lot better than surgery would have, although I should add that when I tell her that, she reminds me that many women have benefitted from reconstructive surgery, and each woman facing that choice has her own set of circumstances.

But I love seeing Sharice in those dresses. The only thing better is seeing her out of them.

She must have been reading my mind because the next things she said was, "I'm going to take a shower. Want to join me?"

I sprinted to open the terrace door. Benz, the smarter of our two four-legged housemates, hissed at Geronimo when the dog hesitated and then shooed him outside and held him at bay while I closed the door. Benz loves to watch the birds. My only theory for Geronimo's dislike of the terrace is he shares my acrophobia.

The routine is obvious – a shared shower then jump in bed and let nature take its course. And it was about to until Sharice whispered something in my ear that caused my nature to take a different course and her to laugh. And she was definitely laughing at me.

"Well," I said, sitting up, "what did you expect to happen when you told me that?"

"I don't know; I've never said that before. But I didn't think it would incapacitate you."

"Only briefly," I said.

We chatted for a moment about her startling announcement.

Then she pushed me back down and sprawled on top of me, and I was right. The incapacity was brief, and nature got back on course.

Afterward, I realized her theory about gruesome things occupying the mind more aggressively than pleasant ones is wrong. Nothing could have occupied my mind more than our interlude in bed.

After we reluctantly put on clothes, Sharice let the animals in and played with them while I sautéed the chopped onions and *calabacitas*, added some garlic and cumin, and then stuffed the mixture into the poblanos. I covered them with Hatch green chile and aged cotija cheese and put the dish in the oven.

Sharice doesn't eat red meat. My challenge is to make dishes for her that also taste good to me. I still eat meat – mostly ground beef in the green chile hamburgers at Blake's and the occasional chorizo breakfast taco – but not when we dine together.

We decided to keep it simple and dine at the coffee table where the rest of the Gruet was still cold. It paired well with the *chiles rellenos,* which were inauthentic because they had not been fried in a batter of egg whites and flour, fried food also being on Sharice's banned food list.

She asked me if I knew about Edith Warner.

"Sure. Most people in New Mexico know about her, especially those who are readers. She was the woman at Otowi Crossing."

"Does *otowi* have a meaning or is it just a name?"

"It's a Tewa word meaning 'where the water makes noise'."

"So the water made noise because the river was shallow, and that's why there was a crossing there?"

"Right. "

"You've been there?"

"Many times."

"Digging for pots?"

"No. It's Indian land. Out of bounds."

"So why did you go there?"

"The guy who lived there with Edith was the uncle of the most famous potter in the history of New Mexico, maybe in the history of the whole country. Her name was Maria Martinez, but most people don't use her last name. If you say you have a pot by Maria, everyone knows who you mean. And they envy you. The cottage Warner lived in and the area around it seem enchanted."

"Well, they are in 'The Land of Enchantment'."

"So claim our license plates. I love to walk along the river bank there."

"Did you know Edith Warner?"

"I'm not *that* old!"

"You'll be fifty on May 5th."

"Thanks for reminding me. Warner died maybe two decades before I was born. Why are we talking about this?"

"Because I cleaned her grandson's teeth today."

"Impossible. Edith Warner had no children."

"How do you know that?"

"Peggy Pond Church."

She frowned. "Let me guess. You looked at the birth and death records in the church Warner attended next to Peggy Pond."

After I stopped laughing, I explained that Peggy Pond Church was the person who wrote a biography of Edith Warner. "It's a great story," I said. "The title is *The House at Otowi Bridge: The Story of Edith Warner and Los Alamos*."

"The guy who claimed to be her grandson seemed genuine, Hubie. Native Americans are generally truthful, right?"

"He was Indian?"

"San Ildefonso," she said, "but he told me he never lived on the reservation."

"Now it gets interesting. Maria's uncle was named Tilano, and he was from San Ildefonso. In fact, he was governor of the Pueblo at one point. But he and Edith never had children."

"They were a couple?"

"Seems no one is certain about that. They lived in the same house for years. Church says they were very fond of each other, but that Warner, even though she was younger than him by a couple of decades, seemed to have more of a maternal concern for him than a romantic one."

"Lots of marriages are like that. My mom sometimes treated dad like her second child. In a cute way, of course. But that doesn't mean there wasn't romance."

"As I recall, Tilano was close to sixty when he moved in."

"People don't stop having sex just because

they get older."

"Good to know," I said. "But people don't have children in their sixties."

"But you just said Warner was younger," she suggested. Then she looked at me and said, "Men can father children at any age."

Which reminded me of her comment in bed which had led to a brief cessation of activity. I suspected she was fishing for further comments from me, but I didn't make any. I needed more time to process the sweet nothing she had whispered.

I thought about my own parents. My mother was in her early forties when I was born. My father was a few years older. They seemed to me to have the perfect partnership. Neither one was in charge. His private world was at the University of New Mexico where he taught. Hers was in the various organizations she belonged to and the activities they engaged in, mostly of a civic nature. Our home was run by Consuela Saenz, maid and nanny. It was clean and orderly, and my parents seemed to be living there as permanent guests, like in the old movies they watched featuring Hammett's Nick and Nora living in a hotel suite. Except Nick and Nora Charles had no children as I recall.

Consuelo Saenz is now Consuelo Sanchez, having married Emilio Sanchez after she moved out of my parents' house when I went to college.

And they have a daughter, Ninfa, who was born shortly afterwards. Consuela was eighteen when she became my niñera (nanny), thirty six when she married Emilio, and thirty eight when they had Ninfa. They never had another child, and Ninfa – although married for many years – has no children. Consuela's main wish at this point is to have a grandchild, but it seems unlikely.

Consuela had serious kidney problems a few years back which worsened to the point that she needed a transplant. I volunteered to be a donor, but tests run on me indicated I was not a suitable donor. Emilio was ruled out as being too old. The perfect donor – not surprisingly – was Ninfa, Consuela's own flesh and blood.

Consuela didn't like the idea because she feared having only one kidney might make it more difficult for Ninfa to carry a baby full-term. I don't think there's any scientific evidence for that, but Consuela relies more on folklore than science.

I like to joke that although my kidney didn't match, my wallet did. I've paid for health care for Consuela and Emilio ever since my parents died. Knowing they would not allow me to do so without good reason, I told them my parents' will provided funds for health insurance for them. If you are unhappy about that white lie, then all I can say is perhaps you need to listen harder to your conscience.

I came out of my brief reverie and said, "There may be some question about whether Warner and Tilano were a couple, but I still doubt that they had a child. That's not something you can hide."

Turns out I was wrong about having children being something you can't hide.

Chapter 5

If you plan to make salsa, you can buy whole tomatoes for about two dollars a pound and dice them up. Or you can buy them already diced for three dollars a pound. The grocery store charges you a buck a pound to do the dicing.

The economics of coffee is different. Sharice pays ten dollars a pound for unroasted coffee beans instead of eight dollars a pound for the same beans already roasted. They charge her for *not* roasting them.

The good thing about those beans is that the aroma of them being roasted is my alarm clock. And I'm in the shower by the time she grinds them, so I avoid the noise of the grinder as well as the howls from Geronimo and the hisses from Benz that the grinder noise elicits.

The coffee also tastes great.

The exercise of the previous evening called for something more substantial than a croissant. I made omelets with the Hatch green chile left over from the *chiles rellenos*. While I toasted a slice of rye bread for Sharice and a corn tortilla for myself, I told her I had a meeting at the university.

"What's the meeting about?"

"Probably not about anything. Academics

love to meet. The start of the spring semester is just an excuse."

"You have to go even though you're just an adjunct?"

I shrugged. "The dean asked me to."

"The dean calls department meetings?"

"Normally it's the department head, but …"

When I didn't finish my sentence, she waited a moment and said softy, "He's dead." After another pause, she added, "Sorry. I guess the less said about that the better."

His name was Milton Shorter. He was shot to death in his office after the end of the fall semester. I was in the office when it happened.

I put my fork down and took a sip of coffee. Jessica Fletcher. Susannah tells me it's more cozy than noir, though I don't know how murder can be cozy. Maybe I should watch an episode. We don't have a television, but evidently you can watch television on a computer these days, and Sharice has one of those.

"Coincidence," she said, reading my mind. Then she leaned over and kissed me on the cheek. "And a lucky one for me. If he hadn't been shot, you'd be dead."

"I try not to think about it."

"You could stay home," she suggested, "and avoid the memories." She smiled and added, "And the weird faculty."

"Some of the faculty are nice. And the weird

ones make the meetings interesting."

"That's the spirit. Got to run." She kissed me again, rubbed Geronimo's head and Benz' ears and headed out.

I took the boys for a walk and washed the dishes when we got back. I cleaned the windows which took a couple of hours because my goal is to make it appear there is no glass in them so that I can enjoy the view of the snow-capped Sandia Mountains to the east.

I left the condo and walked west on Central. Those of you who know Albuquerque realize the university is east of downtown, but the meeting was at three, so I had enough time to go to Treasure House Books in Old Town. I figured the owner, John Hoffsis, would have a copy of *The House at Otowi Bridge.* He specializes in books about The Land of Enchantment.

Since the round-trip walk to Old Town met my daily exercise target, I drove to the university in my old Bronco and actually found a place to park, maybe because the semester hadn't started.

I took the book with me, thinking I might read during the long debates regarding Robert's Rules of Order.

When I arrived at the meeting room adjacent to the dean's office, no one was there. I don't know anything about deans, but artists are not known for punctuality, so I took a seat and started reading the forward of *The House at Otowi Bridge*:

~

I have been sitting in my garden this morning thinking of Edith Warner, how many years it has been since she died and how fast the world we knew has gone on changing. She lies in an Indian grave near the Pueblo of San Ildefonso, nothing over her but the earth hard as a bare heel, and the fragments of the clay pots that were broken over the grave according to the ancient custom of the Pueblo. The little house she lived in beside the bridge was already falling to pieces when I saw it last. The new bridge of towering rigid steel, with two lanes for the traffic that now speeds back and forth to Los Alamos, crosses the Rio Grande close to the wellhouse. The vines that used to hang there, their leaves so glossy and cool in the quivery summer heat, are a mass of clotted dry stems and tendrils. I suppose hardly anyone stops to listen to the river any more.

But I still see Edith standing in the doorway, her thin figure straight as an aspen in a mountain forest, her eyes lifted to the long dark rim of the mesa east of the river. She watches the sky for the northward flight of the wild geese, "that long silver V endlessly circling and reforming," to tell us of spring's sure return.

~

Spring does surely return, bringing new life and – I hoped – helping to put the fall semester out of mind.

Just as the visit of a friend from long ago kindles feelings sweeter than mere memory, so too does the rereading of a good book.

~

I am disappointed when Dean Gangji enters from a side door because I have to close the book.

I stand.

He smiles and extends his right hand. "Hello, Hubert. Thanks for coming." His bright smile softens a stern countenance dominated by a dark full beard and penetrating eyes.

"My pleasure," I reply fatuously. Attending an academic meeting is not a pleasure. Nor is being alone in a room with a person whose rank and demeanor are both intimidating.

"The meeting will begin at 4:00. I asked you to be here at 3:00 so that we could talk before the others arrive."

I wipe a bit of sweat off my upper lip. *Talk about what?* I wonder. The unapproved field trip

I took my students on in the fall? The way I screwed up the budget by not using the clay that had been ordered? The death of one of my students? The sexual harassment complaint? The racial discrimination complaint? The protest my students staged – at my suggestion – that disrupted the student/faculty art show? The department head being shot dead while I was in his office?

Or had Dean Gangji checked the records and wanted now to discuss the fact that I had been expelled from the graduate program in archaeology decades ago for digging up and selling ancient pottery? Running over that list brings to mind seven words: *What the hell am I doing here*?

He asks me to sit down. He turns a chair to face me and sits in it.

"Your first semester as an adjunct was remarkable," he says.

Here comes the list, I think to myself.

He pulls a paper from inside his suit jacket and looks it over. "This is the summary of the numerical portion of the student evaluations of your class in the fall."

I think, *Get this over with.*

"Every one of your students gave you a five in every category. A perfect score."

"That's nice," I mutter.

He reaches into his coat and brings out

another paper. "This is the list of comments they made. Because it is optional, most students don't complete the comments portion of the evaluation. The professors who get comments are the worst and the best. I'm sure you can see why that is the case. The very best professors get positive comments from maybe half their students. But all nine of your students wrote comments. Not just the usual 'Loved this class' or 'Great teacher'. Each one of your students wrote a thoughtful short essay on the positive impact you had on them." He looks up at me and smiles again. "I've been the dean of the college for over a decade. This is the best set of student evaluations I've seen."

I open my mouth. I don't know why; I have nothing to say. Maybe it's my body's reaction to surprise. I finally realize he expects me to comment. I have no idea what to say. The only thing that comes to mind is an explanation – more of an excuse really.

"In the interest of full disclosure, I need to tell you, Dean Gangji, that those positive results may not be an accurate appraisal of me as a teacher. They were achieved under a bizarre set of circumstances that will likely never recur."

"Please elaborate."

"As I'm sure you know, one of my students was murdered. As often happens in tragic circumstances, that brought us all together. We spent most of the semester making ceramics with the idea of selling them and using the proceeds to name a scholarship for the deceased student. So the rave reviews are more about that circumstance than about me."

"I admire your modesty, but it is misplaced. I read every word the students wrote. It is clear that they see you as the person who united them in that shared cause. I would show you what they wrote, but the comments on evaluations are confidential."

"Well, the evaluations are nice. But a class can be evaluated by more than just student opinion." And I recited the litany to him. "What about the unapproved field trip? The way I screwed up the budget by not using the clay that had been ordered? The sexual harassment complaint? The racial discrimination complaint? The protest my students staged – at my suggestion – that disrupted the student/faculty art show? Surely those are not indications of a successful class."

"I appreciate your candor. But in fact, those are all positives. The unapproved field trip was a rousing success according to the students. And the fact that it was unapproved is not your fault. It is ours for not properly orienting you as a new adjunct. The clay was also the department's mistake. You should have been consulted before any supplies were ordered. The two complaints were groundless and both were withdrawn by the students who made them. And in their student evaluation comments, they apologized for filing the complaints in the first place. Frankly, I bear more responsibility than you do because had we made better administrative decisions, none of those things would have happened."

I begin to feel like the guy who is pardoned, given an apology for being unjustly charged and presented with a large check and a cheap suit by way of recompense.

Then I remember the demonstration and disruption my students and I caused at the annual student/faculty art show and mention it to the Dean.

"My favorite part of the story," he says. "That show has been a farce for years. Works get accepted based on petty department politics rather than artistic merit. Your *salon des refusés* was the perfect response. It is time to redo that show and revamp the selection process, and you are the man to do it."

"I don't think the department would let me do that. I'm just an adjunct."

He looks me squarely in the eye. "I am not planning to offer you an adjunct position for the spring semester."

I stare at him. All that praise was just padding for a soft landing after he fires me?

He pulls another paper from his suit jacket; it's like a miniature file system in there. "This is a contract for you as a full-time temp lecturer for the spring semester."

"What's a full-time temp lecturer?"

"It's like an adjunct but full-time. A lecturer is a faculty member who is not eligible for tenure and is usually hired for only one semester. We need someone for the spring semester because, as you know all too well, Junior Prather was dismissed for cause, so we are short one ceramicist."

The "cause" in this case was Junior assaulting me at the aforementioned student/faculty show.

Before proceeding, I feel the need to say a few words about my alma mater lest you get the impression from the foregoing that the crime rate on campus rivals Detroit. For the most part it is an excellent public university with many prestigious faculty members and distinguished graduates. Junior Prather is not one of the former, and I am not one of the latter.

Gangji hands me the contract and says, "You will note that the salary is $24,000. You will teach 4 courses unless you are granted release time for other duties. You will also receive the usual benefit package – health insurance the cost of which is shared between employee and university, and a modest payment into the retirement system. I hope you will agree to the contract."

I do a quick mental calculation. My one course as an adjunct in the fall paid me $2,100. Four courses for $24,000 is $6,000 per course, almost three times the rate per course. My last salaried job was twenty-five years ago. The idea of getting a check every month is irresistible. I sign the contract and hand it back to him.

Chapter 6

After Gangji left, the first faculty member to join me in the dean's conference room was Helga Ólafsdóttir who arrived ten minutes early. Maybe arriving early is important in her native Iceland. Gives you time to warm up before the meeting starts. Helga teaches life drawing and a 3-D studio course where her specialty is weavings.

I suppose Helga belongs to the group of faculty members Sharice described as weird. Depends on whether you think it's weird to pose nude in a class you yourself are teaching so that students can learn figure drawing.

Harte Hockley joined us at 4:00 on the dot. He's a bit conceited, but I don't think conceit is on the weird spectrum. And his high opinion of himself as an artist is justified.

Jollo Bakkie never struck me as the punctual sort, but she was next, perhaps because she is the parliamentarian. I'm told her name is common in Estonia. What is weird is that she is not Estonian. She took some students there on a study-abroad trip and had her name changed after she returned. What didn't change was her aggressive behavior. Jollo teaches water color painting. Except now it is called *aqueous media.*

She longs to teach the real painting course – oil. But Hockley is much better at it. His paintings are displayed at galleries in places like Santa Fe and New York and sell for $10,000. Jollo's paintings are most often seen at Goodwill and priced below five bucks.

Jack Wiezga is a bit eccentric, but the strangest thing about him is he retains a studio in the department even though he has been retired for years. And he has some sort of power over the department. When people in the art department say they wonder which way the wind is blowing, that's code for wondering what Wiezga is thinking.

Next in was Fe Solís who claims to be Native American. I suspect he's a phony. He teaches 'small metals' – formerly known as jewelry making – but the stuff he makes, while showing excellent craftsmanship and design, has no connection to any Native American traditions. And he never mentions any pueblo or tribe. When asked where he grew up, his only remark is, "On a reservation."

Fe was followed closely by an Hispanic woman named Ana Abeyta, a charming person who teaches crafts such as wood carving and Mexican punched tin folk art.

Hal Olley came in with sawdust on his vest. He teaches three sculpting classes – one using metal, one using stone, and one using wood. I assumed he was doing the wood class this semester and had been getting the studio ready. Or maybe the sawdust was left over from a previous course; Hal is habitually messy.

When a tall bespectacled young fellow strolled in, I assumed it was Paul Ethan, the guy who teaches digital art. I never met him in the fall because his classes were all in the evening and he didn't attend departmental meetings, which I took to be a mark in his favor. I'd been told he had a full-time day job doing something with computers.

Melvin Armstrong, the one remaining potter, arrived looking like a man of substance in a well-tailored suit, his beard neatly trimmed, a sheen on his impressive forehead. Because light travels faster than sound, he appears intelligent when he enters a room while speaking. It is only when the sound waves arrive that you realize he is a dunce. He and Junior Prather were so upset by my appointment as an adjunct that they refused to speak to me.

The last person in was Wally Pence, the coordinator of student teaching. He doesn't teach art. He doesn't teach at all. His job is to make the rounds of the public schools where the art education students are doing their practice teaching. He evaluates their progress. If he is weird in some way, I suppose it would be that in his travels around the state, he collects barbed wire and claims to have over a thousand pieces of it taken off of derelict fences. Much of the collection is in his office, which looks like a cactus thicket but less inviting because some of the barbs are eight inches long. And most of the wire is rusted. At least you can't get tetanus from a cactus.

Jollo Bakkie stood up and announced, "In the absence of a department head, it is my job as parliamentarian to call this meeting to order and to chair it until an interim department head is selected. That will be the second item on the agenda. The first is approving the minutes of the last meeting"

"What about tea?" asked Ann Abeyta.

"Please indicate you want be recognized before speaking," Bakkie scolded.

Ann shook her head and raised her hand.

Bakkie said, "The chair recognizes Professor Abeyta."

"What about tea?" asked Abeyta again.

"Organizing tea for the meetings is one of the duties of the department head," Bakkie replied.

"Freddie came up with the idea, and he is now in prison," said Hockley, "and Milton continued it, and he is now dead. Maybe we should abolish the tea serving."

Bakke ruled his comment out of order,

adding, "Tea is not on the agenda. I need a motion to approve the minutes from the last meeting."

"We don't have any minutes to approve," said Helga. "Milton was killed before he had a chance to compile the minutes."

"What about the departmental secretary?" asked Bakkie

"She resigned," said Ann.

"Who could blame her?" Helga said to no one in particular

Bakke glared at her for speaking before being recognized and said, "Under the circumstances, we will follow rule 5.1 C which states that 'At the option of the person chairing a departmental meeting, oral minutes may be approved in lieu of written minutes'. Will someone volunteer to give an oral summary of the last meeting?"

Not surprisingly, no one did.

Finally, Helga raised her hand.

Bakkie said, "Thank you professor Ólafsdóttir. Please give your summary."

Helga said, "The last department meeting was in the fall semester the week before final exams began. There was lengthy discussion on several topics. No decisions were reached."

Some people laughed, Bakke and Armstrong expressed scorn, and everyone started talking at once.

Luckily, I was seated at the back of the room. I opened my book and read Peggy Pond Church's memory of Tilano, Edith Warner's companion and perhaps lover:

~

> Old Tilano, who was nearly sixty when he came across the bridge from the pueblo to live with Edith at "the place where the river makes a noise," comes in from the well and smiles as he sets the bucket of water beside the kitchen door. I shall never forget the gentleness and dignity of his face, brown as a weathered rock, the two black braids of his hair wound with yarn as blue as the sky at midday. I have a picture of him which has stood for a long time on my desk. Dressed in jeans, a sun-faded shirt, a wrinkled cowboy hat, he is stooping to pour clean water over the bare feet of my small son, muddy with play at the edge of the muddy river. The little boy has grown to manhood and has children of his own. Tilano has lived out his life and gone, like Edith, to be part of the timeless spirit of the land. On the high Pajarito Plateau west of the river, where as a child I used to hunt for arrowheads among the pueblo ruins, the city of Los

Alamos now sprawls with its fierce and guarded laboratories, its rows of modern houses, its theaters and flashy supermarkets. The paved road that runs from north to south across the plateau parallels the remnants of an old trail worn ankle-deep in places by the moccasined feet of Indians. On one side of the road is a tightly woven metal fence bearing in enormous red letters the warning DANGER! PELIGROSO! On the other, a "sacred area" has been set aside where the Indians of San Ildefonso still tend traditional shrines and place prayer plumes when their hearts are right.

~

I am jolted back to the present when I hear my name. They have finally done something about the minutes and have turned to the selection of an interim department head.

Helga has nominated *me*.

Armstrong is on his feet. "He can't serve as interim head. He's just an adjunct."

"No," replies Helga. "Dean Gangji issued him a contract as a full-time temp to replace Junior Prather. As a full-time faculty member, he is eligible to serve as interim head."

"Outrageous," yells Armstrong. "He doesn't even have a degree in art."

"Neither do I," says Ann Abeyta. "But I am more acclaimed as an artist than most people who do have degrees. Hubie is a skilled potter, much better than the person he is replacing."

"Nonsense," says Armstrong. "Junior was a fine potter and a good colleague. Schuze is a criminal!"

Bakke is yelling for order, but no one is paying attention.

Hockley chimes in. "You seem confused, Melvin. Junior is the criminal. He pled guilty to assaulting Hubie and escaped a jail term only because Hubie agreed to probation in the sentencing hearing."

"But Schuze is a pot thief!" Melvin is now shaking and pointing a finger at me.

"He has never been convicted of a crime," Hockley responds calmly.

"Only because he hasn't been caught."

True, I think to myself. But the more pressing issue is why Helga would nominate me as interim chair. Given her low opinion of most of her colleagues, she probably did it just to rankle them. But why would Abeyta and Hockley come to my defense unless they thought the nomination was serious? And now I hear Wally Pence seconding the promotion.

"Are there any further nominations?" asks Bakkie.

Armstrong shouts, "I nominate myself."

"Professor Armstrong has been nominated," says Bakke, happy to be back in control. "Is there a second?"

Melvin's head swings back and forth, spittle flying from his drooping jaw.

"The nomination of Professor Armstrong dies for lack of a second," says Bakkie. "Are there any further nominations?"

Melvin stomps out.

"Seeing as how there is only one nominee," says Helga, "I move that we select Hubert Schuze by acclamation as interim department head for the spring semester."

"I have not recognized you," says Bakke.

"Sure you have. I'm the gorgeous tall blond from Iceland."

The gorgeous part is true. The tall part is true. The blond part is mostly true; there is a lot of grey mixed in. She must be close to fifty, but she is lean, fit and energetic. And the waiting list for her figure drawing class – almost all young males – would fill the Lobo football stadium. Which is more than can be said about the football team.

Bakkie rolls her eyes and says, "Professor Ólafsdóttir has the floor."

Helga repeats her motion to elect me by acclamation. Ana seconds Helga's motion, Bakkie calls for a vote, and in less time than it would have taken me to read another page of

The House at Otowi Bridge, I am now interim head of the art department.

Chapter 7

I walked west on Central in a daze. I walked past the old Albuquerque High School I graduated from long ago. It has been converted to condos. I passed under Interstate 25. I looked to the left and spotted a RailRunner boarding passengers at the train station. I came to the Kimo Theater and noticed that *Tarde de Oro*, a musical about Albuquerque's history, was being presented again. The familiar landmarks were reassuring and seemed to help me out of my daze.

I started thinking about Edith Warner. And continued doing so until I reached *Dos Hermanas* where I hoped sanity might be restored. Or, failing that, where it might be drowned.

Susannah saw me arrive from the direction of Central. When I sat down, she asked, "Where's the Bronco?"

It seemed an odd question until I remember I drove to the university.

"I left it at the university."

"Why?"

I shook my head. "Because I forgot it was there."

"Early onset Alzheimer's," she said and signaled Angie to bring two margaritas.

"I usually walk there, so naturally I just walked back like I normally do."

"Lame excuse."

"I have a better one."

"Which is?"

"I was there for a meeting of the art faculty. The main agenda item was selection of an interim head of the department."

"Because Shorter is dead."

"Why does everyone keep mentioning that? I know he's dead. I was in his office when his brains were blown out!"

"Geez, Hubie. Don't bite my head off. You *do* need a drink."

"Sorry."

And right on cue, Angie arrived and placed the one with a salted rim in front of me and the one without in front of Susannah. She centered the chips and *pico de gallo* on the table.

Susannah loaded a chip with *pico de gallo* and held it up – elbow on the table, chip in the air – as she often does, as if doing so somehow enhances the taste. Maybe it's a gender thing. When I scoop up *pico de gallo* or salsa, I immediately eat it.

"So what's the good excuse you have for forgetting the Bronco?"

"They elected me interim department head."

Her loaded chip dropped to the table, and

some of the salsa ended up on the side of my margarita glass. I licked it off and washed it down with the best swallow I ever had. Or maybe just the one I have needed more than any other.

"An adjunct can't be department head," she asserted.

"I'm no longer an adjunct; I'm a full-time temp lecturer."

"When did that happen?"

"Dean Gangji met with me alone just before the meeting. He said I had the best student evaluations he's ever seen."

"He gave you a full-time appointment just because you got good students evals?"

"And also because they need another ceramicist since Junior Prather—"

"Was fired for assaulting you."

I nodded, staying calm this time about her finishing my sentence.

"Did you want to be department head?"

"The thought never crossed my mind."

"Then why did you take it?"

"I didn't take it. It was thrust on me."

"Right. A groundswell."

"More like an unexpected tidal wave. I was sitting at the back of the room. First they debated whether to serve tea. Then they debated the minutes of the last meeting. Despite such weighty matters hanging in the balance, I started reading my book. Then I heard Helga nominate me. By the time I caught on to what was happening, it was done."

"Are you prepared to do the job?"

"No."

"So you have a job you didn't seek and are not prepared to do."

"Exactly."

"You'll have to tell them you decided not to accept the job."

"That's what I thought at first. But then I started thinking about Edith Warner. You know who she is?"

"Of course I do. We read about her in the 8th grade. She's one of my heroes."

"Then you know that, like me, she got a job she didn't want and wasn't suited for."

"She mothered all the weird male scientists at Los Alamos while they were making the atom bomb. They made her chocolate cake famous in their various memoirs. That hardly required an MBA. Any woman of gumption could have done it."

"I'm talking about the job she had before that."

"Which was?"

"Freight agent and post mistress. The house where she eventually ran a tea room, baked cakes, and mothered all those scientists was next to a stop on the Denver & Rio Grande narrow-gauge railroad. Years before the Manhattan Project, that station was where all the mail and supplies arrived for the San Ildefonso Pueblo, the Los Alamos School, and the handful of farmers and prospectors scattered across Pajarito Mesa. The cargo was unloaded into a small shed where it stayed until people came to pick it up. Most of it was for the school which sent a truck down to Otowi three times a week. Someone had to live there to handle mail and to oversee the unloading of the freight and keep watch over it."

"That was a job she didn't want and wasn't suited for?"

"Yep. She was a sickly young woman sent west in the hope that the dry air would bolster her health. She fell in love with New Mexico and was determined not to return east. But the money her family gave her for the trip was running out. Then, like in my case, fate took a hand."

"Oh brother. First the job was thrust on you. Now it's fate."

"Right, it was fate that did the thrusting. In Warner's case, it was a chance meeting with the guy who ran the Los Alamos School. He was desperate to find someone to mind the freight at Otowi because the last guy who had the job disappeared. And you might be interested in him."

"Sure, why not? A lot of men I've known have disappeared. What was interesting about him?"

"He was Basque. He was a retired lumberjack, and his name was Shorty."

"Doesn't compute. First, Basques don't name their sons 'Shorty'. Second, they were herders, not lumberjacks. And third, if he were a lumberjack, he wouldn't have made enough money to retire during the Great Depression."

"Maybe they called him Shorty because he was a Basque-ette. Get it?"

"Groan."

I returned to my story and told her that when Warner told the guy who ran the school that she wanted to stay in New Mexico but couldn't, he tried to convince her to take the freight job.

"Listen to this great passage," I said and pulled the book out of my pocket:

~

> "You can rent the house for very little," he told her. "María and Julián own it. Their son, Adam, will come over to unload the freight for you. All you have to do is see that he gets there on time. We will pay you twenty-five dollars a month." He sounded as though he thought it was a princely sum. At least it would be better than

nothing, she told herself. With her long experience in frugal living she might make it do. "That will cover the rent and Adam's wages," Mr. Connell continued. Edith's heart sank. How did he expect her to live, she wondered? Did he think the birds would feed her? "Of course the profits of the store will all be yours," he had added quickly. "And with you living there, no one will attempt theft." Surely desperation had addled his wits a little, she thought. Frail and reticent as she had always been, how could anyone possibly take her for a watchdog? At the bridge she would be entirely alone except for the few passersby, Indians, sheepherders, an occasional tourist, no other human being within shouting distance, not even a telephone except the railway instrument which was unavailable for private use. Her only link with the world would be the truck from the school, and the trains that often whistled past without stopping. Her nearest neighbors would be the Indians at the pueblo, a long walk on the other side of the river. The whole plan seemed completely fantastic. Surely there could be no one as little suited for such a job. Yet to wait for another opportunity

> would be too great a gamble. The meager resources with which her family had been helping through her illness had been exhausted. A decision had to be made at once. Return east she would not, of that much she was certain. This offer would tide her over for a little, would give her time to look for a better solution. "How soon can you take over?" the determined voice was asking. "I can start any time," she heard herself say, amazed, as though she listened to some stranger.

~

"See the similarity? I can no more be a department head than she could be a watchdog. But fate foisted those jobs on us in the guise of Connell in her case and Helga in mine. And I thought if a frail young woman can succeed as a watch dog and railroad agent in the wilds of New Mexico in the 1930s, I can surely succeed as a department head in the twenty-first century."

"What does the twenty-first century have to do with it?"

"She didn't even have a telephone!"

"Neither do you."

"Of course I do. You've called me on it many times."

"That's a land line in your shop. Since you moved in with Sharice, you might as well be in the witness protection program. You need a cell phone."

We've had fun with the cell phone argument for years. To me they're like that chip people have a vet implant in their dog so they'll always be able to find rover when he's roving. The phone company knows where you are and who you talk to twenty-four seven, three hundred and sixty five.

She had another loaded chip in the air and was thinking. "Was the dean at the meeting?"

"No."

"Then how did the faculty know you were eligible to be interim head?"

"Helga Ólafsdóttir told them."

"But you said the dean gave you the new position right before the meeting. How would Helga have known about it?"

Good question, I thought to myself.

"I'll tell you how," she said. "It was a set up, and Helga was in on it."

"I don't get it."

"Only the dean could have managed this. In theory, he could have gone to the meeting and announced that he was appointing you interim head. Deans have the authority to appoint department heads, especially interim ones, without any consultation, but it's bad politics to do that. So he arranged for the faculty to elect you."

"Hmm. You might be right. As I understand it, Pakistan is an authoritarian place, but also full of political intrigue. So it might fit with Gangji's background."

"Gangji is from India."

"But his first name is Mohammed."

"There are Muslims in India, Hubert."

"Oh, right."

"So," she explained, "Gangji tells Helga in advance that he is going to make you a full-time temp so that she can inform the faculty at the meeting. And he must have talked to some of the others, maybe even most of them, to make sure they would support the plan. How many of them voted for you?"

"All of them. It was by acclamation. Well, except for Armstrong who had stomped out of the meeting before the vote was taken."

"There you have it. It was a backroom deal."

I was about to challenge her explanation as a typical conspiracy theory when proof that she was correct walked into *Dos Hermanas* in the guise of Helga Ólafsdóttir, Harte Hockley, Ana Abeyta and Wally Pence.

"We've come to congratulate our new interim department head," said Ana as they pulled chairs up to our table.

Angie showed up without being summoned and said, "I'm assuming two bottles of Gruet Blanc de Noir?"

"Double that," said Harte, and everyone nodded agreement.

After the Gruet was poured, Harte raised his glass and said. "To our new department head. Best of luck."

"He'll need it," said Helga, and everyone laughed. Even me, but only to be polite.

"Hubie," said Wally, "want to say a few words?"

"Yes. Why did you do this to me?"

After the laughter died down, Ana said, "We knew the only persons who would want the job were Armstrong and Bakke. She couldn't nominate herself since she chairs the meetings, and we knew no one else would. So that would leave Armstrong as the only contender. We needed another candidate. But no one else was willing to do it. Then Helga suggested you. It made sense except for the fact that you were an adjunct. So Helga convinced the dean to make you a full-time temp. The official reason is to replace Junior Prather. But the real reason is so you can serve as head while we run a search. We hope to attract some good candidates."

"And the dean went along with it?"

They eyed each other. Harte was the one who finally spoke. "Gangji tried to get Helga to do it. Then he tried me. He was about to try Wally when we just laid it on the line and said none of us would do it."

Not exactly what Susannah had guessed, but close enough. All the buttering up about my student evaluations was just window dressing. So what? I still had the salary, and that was good. And I still had no idea how to be a department head, and that was bad.

Susannah said, "Hubie was telling me before you arrived that he has no idea how to be a department head."

They all laughed, and Helga said, "Neither did the last two guys."

"It's an impossible job," said Harte. "The faculty are all tenured, so you have virtually no influence on them. They theoretically report to you, but you're actually like the guy who mows the cemetery – there are a lot of people under you, but none of them are listening."

"Don't worry," said Ana. "We'll help you."

Chapter 8

Susannah offered to drive me to the university to retrieve the Bronco, but I told her just to drop me at the condo.

Sharice looked at me and said, "Did someone die?"

"I look that bad?"

"You look shell-shocked."

"I guess I am."

She led me to the love seat. "What happened?"

"I was elected interim head of the art department."

A hurt look slid onto her face. "Why didn't you tell me you applied for that?"

"Because I didn't apply. I'd never do anything like that before talking it over with you."

Her smile reappeared and she squeezed my hand. "Okay. This is exciting. How did you get the job without applying for it?"

"Helga Ólafsdóttir nominated me for it. No one else was nominated except for Melvin Armstrong who nominated himself. No one seconded his nomination. So I got it by default."

"So the black guy who's been teaching there for years loses to a new whitey who's just an adjunct. The diversity police are going to be all over that."

"I don't think it had anything to do with—"

"I'm just kidding. You know what I think of Armstrong. He was horrible to you."

"True. But it wasn't because I'm white. He loved Junior Prather who's even whiter than I am."

"There are shades of white?"

I stuck out my arm and pulled hers alongside it. "I'm almost as dark as you are. Unlike me, Prather is pasty."

Doing her imitation of Butterfly McQueen, Sharice said, *"I's a light-skinned colored girl and you's a tan-skinned white boy. We's made fo one nother.* But seriously, you should wear sunscreen. It's not healthy to be exposed to that much UV radiation."

"It's not all UV. My skin is a bit tan even on the parts of me that don't get sunlight."

"I know. I like those parts." Then she laughed and said, "And I like when your skin turns red."

"I'm not blushing. It's just the effect of too much Gruet." I told her about the impromptu celebration at *Dos Hermanas*.

"Too bad. Gruet would be great with what I fixed for dinner tonight."

"I don't smell anything."

"That's because it's a salad. Kale, apple

slices, dried mangos with smoked paprika, and an avocado lemon vinaigrette."

"Yum," I deadpanned.

She poked me and said, "You love green vegetables."

"Yes. Poblanos, jalapenos, serranos, tomatillos, noplalitos—"

"Shut up and come to the table."

My own cooking is based on what Consuela fed me for the first eighteen years of my life. Putting smoked paprika on dried mangos sounded like wearing brown shoes with a tux. But they were the highlight of the salad and would have paired well with some Gruet, but I'd already had three glasses. Okay, maybe four.

After changing into her pajamas, Sharice said we were moving to the couch for dessert. She brought flans and told me I could have a small coupe of champagne with dessert.

When we finished, she slid next to me and asked if I had thought about what she had whispered to me in bed.

I can't explain it without telling you what she said, but I'm a bit uncomfortable with the topic.

She said we were about to have unprotected sex.

Which caused me briefly to be ... er, physically unable to do so.

I associate the phrase 'unprotected sex' with

the AIDs epidemic. So I had reminded her that I was the only person she'd ever had sex with, and I hadn't had sex for a couple of years before she and I got together. So there was no way she could have an STD, and if I had one, symptoms would have shown up well before two years passed.

But it was not protection from STDs that she had in mind. It was protection from pregnancy.

You may recall my mentioning that she and I discussed it briefly and then got back to nature taking its course. The gist of that discussion was that neither of us had any objection to being parents and were happy to let fate decide whether that came to pass.

Being an old-fashioned guy raised by old-fashioned parents, my real view was that we should get married before we made a baby. But I didn't want to use the intimate occasion to ask her once again. I had pestered her about it too often. And I knew she was struggling to balance her desire for us to be a normal couple with the promise she had made to her father not to marry a white man

I'd had enough time to think it out. "I'd be delighted if you got pregnant," I said. "This business with the dead guy in the plaza has me thinking about family. You and I are a family of sorts even though we aren't yet married. We'd be even more of a family with a child."

"You know I want to be with you forever. It's just that ..."

"You promised your dad you'd never marry a white guy."

She nodded and said, "Maybe he'd change his mind if I were pregnant. I wonder if that was in my subconscious when I decided to forego birth control."

"Maybe he'd want you to get an abortion."

She slid even closer to me. "I've always been pro-choice. We women have the right to control our own bodies. But if it was your baby inside me, I couldn't abort it. Does that make me a hypocrite?"

"Of course not. Being pro-choice doesn't mean you favor abortions. It just means you favor women making the decision."

"You're sure you don't have any reservations about becoming a father?" she asked. And then added, "If it happens."

"Not any big ones. I guess I worry about being a new father at fifty. Actually, it's not that. It's more about being almost seventy by the time she graduates from high school."

"Why 'she'."

I smiled at her. "Because the more frequently a couple have sex, the more likely they are to conceive a girl."

"That sounds like an old wives' tale."

"Nope. Scientific fact. A biologist named

Landrum Shettles discovered back in the sixties that couples who have sex frequently are more likely to have girls, and couples who have sex less frequently are more likely to have boys."

"You should go on Jeopardy."

Constant reading has filled my head with a lot of useless information.

"Do you have a preference?" she asked.

"Yes. I prefer more frequently."

She laughed and asked, "Boy or girl?"

"No preference. But I hope we don't have twins."

"Why?"

"Because how can you breast feed two babies with one breast?"

When she stopped laughing, she lifted her pajama top just a few inches and said, "It's only one, but it's perfect. Want a peek?"

And our odds of conceiving a girl were increased a short while later.

Chapter 9

After Sharice left for work early the next morning, I washed the dishes, walked the boys, and returned to see Agent Charles Webbe guarding the condo.

In fact, he was merely waiting for me, but he is incapable of a waiting pose. He is constantly alert and vigilant, almost certainly a result of his training at the FBI Academy. And at 6′ 3″ and 225 pounds of muscle, he would make an excellent guard.

"You ever heard of the Jessica Fletcher Syndrome?" I asked him after we were inside and coffee had been poured.

"Sure. From *Murder She Wrote*. And you have the syndrome."

"Come on. You don't really believe in that, do you?"

"I didn't until I met you."

Charles' glare is enough to make children cry and innocent men confess. But when he smiles, he looks like a giant black teddy bear.

"You here because of the guy they found in Old Town?"

He nodded

"You don't want me to go to the morgue, do you?"

"No. What I want is a lot simpler. But it may sound unusual and even a bit weird. I want a sample of your DNA."

I felt light-headed and put both hands on the table to steady myself. "Why?"

He handed me a snapshot. It was me in my bank.

"Who took this?" I asked.

"The security camera. It's you, right?"

I looked down at it again. "Not a great picture, but it's me."

He handed me a second snapshot. "What about this one?"

It was me in my Bronco. But the picture wasn't clear. I'm not sure I would have known it was me except for the fact that there aren't many 1985 Broncos still running.

"Yeah, that's also me. Am I under surveillance?"

He laughed. "These days, everyone is. That picture was taken by a traffic camera."

"This is scary."

"I know. Like a lot of modern technology, it can have great benefits and also scary downsides."

"What are the benefits of secretly taking pictures of bank customers?"

"None. Until one of them pulls a pistol out of a deposit bag and robs the bank."

"Surely I'm not a suspect in a bank

robbery!"

"You are not. And if the person in that picture had in fact robbed that bank, I would have begun my investigation with the assumption that it wasn't you but someone cleverly disguised as you."

"Because you know I'm a law-abiding citizen."

"No. You break the law every time you dig up an old pot. But you don't have the *cojones* for bank robbery."

I nodded and we both laughed.

"These pictures are the reason you want my DNA?"

"I prefer not to tell you the reason at this point. I know how you are, Hubie. Do us both a favor and don't obsess on this. Just keep these two things in mind. First, no one outside of law enforcement knows about this; don't say anything except to Sharice. Second, I'm here as a friend."

Chapter 10

On Thursday evenings, Dr. Santiago Batres provides free dental care for indigent residents of Albuquerque. Given that my hometown has the fifth highest poverty level in the country, the lines are always long. Sharice donates her time like the doc does, but he gives her comp time to make up for it.

Santiago and I were in the same graduating class from Albuquerque High School. He was a star on the football team. I was the top student in math. He became a respected dentist. I became a pot thief. If there is a sociological message there, I don't want to know it.

I often spend Thursday evenings at *Dos Hermanas* with Susannah and other drinking buddies who happen by. The tradition began many years ago when I was living behind my shop and Susannah was waiting tables two blocks away at La Placita. She was often my server when I ate there but only at lunch because in the evenings she was taking courses at the University. Her shift got prolonged one day when she didn't happen to have a class, and she dropped by *Dos Hermanas* after work because she also didn't happen to have a date.

The only single guy there was someone she

already knew – me. I invited her to join me and bought her a margarita. When I asked her why I'd never seen her there before, she said she was always in class or on a date.

"And tonight?" I asked.

"No class tonight, and I'm between boyfriends."

I pretended be to confused, looked around the table and said, "I don't see the other one."

She laughed and said, "I'm in my early twenties" in a putting-the-cards-on-the-table tone.

"I'm in my early forties."

"You look a lot younger."

"Okay, I'm really only twenty-eight, but I didn't want you to get your hopes up."

"Because you already have a girlfriend?"

I shook my head.

"So you're between girlfriends?"

"Depends. I had a girlfriend a few years ago. So this won't technically be a 'between' period unless I find another one."

"You're funny. Are you really in your forties."

"I am. Too old for you?"

"Not at this point. But in twenty years …"

The unfinished sentence hung in the air until I finally said, "You'll be a sexy forty something, and I'll be preparing to file for Social Security."

"Friends?" she asked, and held up her margarita.

We clinked glasses to seal the deal. I wondered for a few months whether if I had pushed a bit, we might have become more than friends. Does age really matter? Sharice is about halfway between Susannah and me in terms of age. But Sharice and Susannah are close friends, and Sharice and I are a couple.

After Susannah and I had clinked glasses, I pressed my upper lip against my teeth and mimicked, "this could be the beginning of a beautiful friendship."

She laughed and said, "That didn't sound like Bogart."

"Sure it did. Otherwise, how would you know who I was imitating?"

"I know the line. I've watched *Casablanca* maybe a hundred times."

It *has* been a beautiful friendship. But also a painful one because I've had to help her cope with a series of disastrous romances. So now you understand why, when she and I were discussing Shorty who disappeared from Otowi, she said, "A lot of men I've known have disappeared."

Which makes no sense because she is tall, shapely, and pretty. More importantly, she has a great sense of humor and is fun to be around. I'll admit she isn't frilly, and I guess that bothers some guys. Susannah's idea of ranch dressing is boots, jeans, and a cowboy hat. She rides horses, ropes goats, and castrates calves, skills that are valued in New Mexico, although the last one is probably not something to be mentioned on a first date.

It's now almost a decade later, and all those evening courses paid off last year when she received a master of arts degree in art history. There aren't many jobs for people with an M.A. in art history, so she's still waitressing at La Placita. She tells me the money's good, and the best thing is the flexible schedule. She can take a few days off to spend with her family on their ranch near Willard.

She was again between boyfriends. But one of the previous ones was about to make a reappearance. Frederick Blass, former head of the Art Department, was scheduled to be released from the State Penitentiary at noon the next day.

I never took an art class when I was a student at UNM. I didn't even know where the art building was. But when Freddie invited Susannah to a party at his penthouse, she took me as a faux date because she wasn't sure whether he had invited her as a date or merely a guest. No way I could have anticipated that I'd end up with his job.

It turned out to be a fun evening at Freddie's

until Jessica Fletcher struck. Someone was killed in the building, and I became a suspect.

But Freddie was the guilty party. His plea of self-defense didn't get him acquitted, but it must have influenced the jury and judge because he got a light sentence.

After visiting him in prison last year, I decided no sentence is *light*. The guy Susannah had fallen for was tall, dark and handsome – wavy black hair, sharp nose and intelligent eyes.

The guy I saw at the penitentiary had white hair, a broken nose, and sunken eyes. Intelligence still shone in the background. Or perhaps *wisdom* is a better word for it.

He taught painting to the other inmates. The warden commended him for doing so, saying it was therapeutic.

He gave me a sketch he made of Susannah. The way he held the paper – gently, the way a Buddhist monk might hold a rice paper lantern – told me he was still in love with her.

When I gave Susannah that sketch last year, she stared at it and said, "*Dance in the Country*."

Turns out it was based on a painting by Renoir of two young people on a picnic in the countryside who have impetuously decided to dance rather than eat. The girl in Freddy's version is Susannah. She was touched by the drawing, but not moved when I told her Freddy was a changed man.

"They all say that to the parole board," she said.

Freddie was now being released, and I sat there wondering how to broach the subject again. I didn't want to be his advocate. But I thought he deserved a second chance at life. And with Susannah? I didn't know. I decided the best tack was just to tell her I was his ride.

"I'm picking up Freddie tomorrow and bringing him to Albuquerque."

"And you're telling me why?"

"Don't want you to be shocked if you see him on the street."

"I can always cross to the other side."

That went well, I thought to myself.

She said, "Let's change the subject to something I'm interested in."

"Okay, how about Charles Webbe coming to the condo to get a DNA sample from me?"

"A murder mystery! That's more like it. Why did he want your DNA?"

"He wouldn't tell me. And he told me not to tell anyone except Sharice."

She looked at her arm. "Nope, not Sharice – I'm still a white girl."

We laughed so hard that it took me a few seconds to realize there was a third laugher behind me.

Martin Seepu came around my right side, sat down and rolled up a sleeve to expose his arm. "Looks like I'm also still a redskin. What about you, paleface?"

I rolled up a sleeve. "I'm still a Mounds candy bar – brown on the outside and white on the inside."

"You and about a million other New Mexicans," he said to me. Then he asked Susannah why she checked to make sure she wasn't black.

"Hubie just told me about Charles Webbe asking him for a DNA sample. He told Hubie not to tell anyone about it except for Sharice."

"I've heard Charles explain that," said Martin. "He says there should be no secrets between people who sleep together."

Susannah said, "Hubie and I don't sleep together."

"But you're as close as people who do," Martin replied.

If you're wondering why Martin and I had to roll up our shirtsleeves, the answer is neither of us owns a short-sleeve shirt. Next time you pass a field where migrant workers are harvesting vegetables, note they all wear long-sleeve shirts. It's cooler in the desert with your arms covered.

Other than long-sleeve shirts, Martin and I didn't have much in common when we met. He was fourteen, and I was an undergraduate who signed up for a mentoring program on the reservations. A guy from Student Services drove a van full of Hispanic and Anglo middle-class kids from the university out to Martin's pueblo and ushered us into a rec center that had the acoustic quality of a concrete culvert. After making some remarks no one could hear, he handed each college student a name tag and told us to hang it around our neck. Then he went outside to smoke.

Each of the Indian kids had a slip of paper with the name of one of the mentors. It reminded me of a school dance at the end of the year in my eighth-grade class. The boys were led into the gym single-file on one side. The girls came in on the other side. We guys were instructed that when the music began, we were to cross the gym and say to the girl directly across from us, "May I have this dance?"

It worked about as poorly as you'd imagine. The girl across from me repositioned herself to avoid me. After some hesitation, I veered to the left only to discover that Eloise Wainwright was the only girl remaining in that area. Eloise was a bright girl. She was also a head taller than me. And her father was the principal.

I suspect today's students don't have to endure the angst we suffered back then. For one thing, a dance arranged as a boy/girl event would likely encounter protests from LGB advocates. Maybe college kids mentoring Indian kids is also politically incorrect these days. And don't tell me 'Indian' is politically incorrect. It's the term Martin and everyone else in his pueblo use. He told me early on that 'Native American' makes no sense. First, America was named for Amerigo Vespucci, an Italian, and as Martin quipped, "My people don't do spaghetti." And 'native' is derived from the Latin word for birth. But the peoples who were here when the Europeans arrived do not see their connection with this land as an accident of birth. They are part of the land like the trees, animals, rivers and mountains.

Martin had drawn my name. "Why did you volunteer?" he asked.

"One of my professors suggested it. What about you?"

"My dad made me do it. What did the professor teach?"

"Math. You like math?"

"Yes."

"What part do you like best?"

"Graphs."

We found some paper, and I gave him a couple of equations that generated irregular curves. He graphed them perfectly. Taking a wild leap, I asked him if he could figure out how to calculate the area under one of those curves. He didn't know the exact procedure of course, but his explanation of how it might be done was brilliant. So I decided to teach him calculus.

He taught me how to draw horses in motion. We bonded over skills neither of us has any use for. Turns out the most important thing we have in common is the belief that it is better to know than not to know, even if you never use the knowledge.

We are like family now. His sister Sunny made my special jacket. Not because I asked her to. Not because it was my birthday. But because she thought I needed it. Martin's uncle is a gifted potter and sells his works through Spirits in Clay. Edith Warner said about her friend Maria, "It matters not that the color of skin be different, that language be not the same, that even the gods of our fathers be known by a different name. We are people, the same kind of human beings who live and love and go on, and I find myself ever forgetting that my friends are known as Indians and I am a white woman born. Perhaps that is why we are neighbors, even down in our hearts."

I asked Martin what brought him to town.

"My feet," he deadpanned. Then he said, "I'm now a volunteer docent at The Indian Pueblo Cultural Center. Just finished telling a busload of palefaces about the 19 different pueblos in New Mexico, and listening to one of them complain about the word *Indian* being in the name of the place. Fighting political correctness is thirsty work, so I stopped by figuring you'd buy me a beer."

"Why should I pay for it?" I asked.

"*Noblesse oblige.*"

"Since when did I become part of the privileged class?"

"All the descendents of the Europeans who invaded this continent became the privileged class when they put us on reservations."

"Okay, I'll buy that. And a beer for you."

He smiled and said, "It's good to be a silver-throated orator."

I asked Angie to bring him a Tecate.

Martin asked me why Charles wanted my DNA.

"He wouldn't tell him," Susannah answered for me, "but I know why. He wants to compare it to some DNA they found on the dead guy Hubie found in the Plaza."

"I didn't *find* him. I just happened to pass by after he'd already been found and the ambulance and police were already there."

"That might make sense for mister average citizen," she replied, "but for someone with the Jessica Fletcher Syndrome, there are no coincidental bodies. It's all part of a pattern."

I'd decided not to rise to any further Jessica Fletcher comments, so I noted that since I hadn't touched anything, none of my DNA could be on the dead guy.

"It wouldn't have to be yours," she said. "It could be from Benz."

Martin and I looked at each other and then turned to her and said in unison, "Huh?"

"DNA from a cat solved a murder in Britain," she said by way of explanation, although I failed to see anything explanatory in her sentence.

"Sounds like something from one of those Lilian Braun Jackson *The Cat Who* books," said Martin.

I looked at him and said – by myself this time – "Huh?"

He said, "A series of murder mystery novels where the protagonist's cat solves the mysteries."

"That makes perfect sense. What doesn't make sense is you reading murder mysteries. Why didn't I know that?"

"I'm not proud of it. Shows the power of the dominant culture."

Angie brought his beer. He took a sip and said, "The early books in that *Cat Who* series were good. But when she had the protagonist leave the city and move to Moose County, they went downhill."

"I think they got better," said Susannah.

"They were silly," said Martin. "The towns in Moose County had names like Brrr, Chipmunk, and Flapjack."

"And there are towns in New Mexico called Pie Town, Elephant Butte and Truth or Consequences. But that doesn't make the state silly."

"Can we get back to the cat DNA thing?" I asked.

"Sure," said Susannah. "A few years ago, British police found a dismembered torso wrapped in a shower curtain. There were no fingerprints or anything else in the way of clues except for some cat hairs on the curtain. The DNA in those hairs was found to match the DNA of a cat named Tinker, and that led to a conviction."

"They convicted Tinker of murder?"

"Don't be ridiculous. They convicted his owner."

"So what does that have to do with Benz?"

"The suspect in Britain probably washed the curtain or rubbed it to make sure his prints weren't on it. But cat hair sticks to things. So maybe the police here in Albuquerque also found cat hairs on the dead guy in the Plaza."

"But Charles didn't get a DNA sample from Benz. He got it from *me*."

"If you read murder mysteries, Hubie, this would all be obvious to you. My guess is the dead guy in the Plaza had cat hair on him. But he didn't own a cat. So the cat hair was transferred to him by contact with another human who does have a cat. Call him Cat Man. So the cat hair has a trace of Cat Man's DNA on its surface which resulted from Cat Man petting his cat."

I gave my head a quick shake and asked, "How do we know the dead guy didn't have a cat?"

"We need to stop calling him *the dead guy*," she said. "Sounds disrespectful."

"We don't know his name."

"So let's give him one."

"How about Gurney Guy?" Martin suggested. "So how do we know Gurney Guy didn't own a cat?"

"Simple," said Susannah, "If he did, the police wouldn't be trying to figure out where the cat hair came from. They'd just figure it was from his cat."

"Actually," I said, "they may have had good reason for thinking the cat hair wasn't from his cat even if he *did* have one. Whit told me he was a snappy dresser, wore expensive suits, had a silk handkerchief in the breast pocket of his jacket, and had manicured nails. A guy like that would have brushed off any pet hairs before going out."

"So there you have it," she said and sat back in her chair. "You pet Benz, some of his hair sticks to your hand. You walk by Gurney Guy, a few of the cat hairs float over and land on him, and the next thing you know, you're a person of interest."

Then it dawned on me. "Impossible. Gurney Guy was completely covered by a sheet."

I don't know which made me feel better, escaping the fear that Benz had linked me to Gurney Guy or getting out of that ridiculous conversation.

Then I remembered the crumpled paper Whit showed me. He'd said not to worry about my prints being on it after I handled it. They had already looked for prints and found none. They would know my prints, if any, were added after the death. But had they subsequently examined that paper for DNA and found some on it? And if it was mine, how would I be able to prove the DNA wasn't on it *before* Whit handed it to me? He'd said, "You know I'm a better cop than that." I was hoping that was true. And that I didn't become Cat Man.

"Being as you two are murder mystery readers," I said, "maybe you can explain something Whit told me. A tourist was using his phone to make a video of Old Town Plaza and happened to capture Gurney Guy as he fell over and died. The cause of death is presumed to be a puncture wound in his back that led to him bleeding to death. There were other people in the Plaza, but none of them close enough to stab him. Whit was hoping I could figure it out because he said I have an 'encyclopedia mind'."

"I can explain it *Kemo Sabe,*" said Martin deadpan. "Bow and arrow. Show me the feathers on the shaft, and I'll tell you who did it."

"That's the problem. There was nothing in or around the wound. No bullet, no sharp object, nothing."

"I've got it," said Susannah. "An icicle."

"An icicle?"

"Yes," she said, "Simon Brett called it the perfect murder weapon."

I looked at Martin, and he said, "A famous murder mystery writer and my personal favorite. He wrote the Charles Paris and Mrs. Pargeter series among others."

I was still having a hard time picturing Martin reading murder mysteries.

Susannah said, "The icicle is perfect because you stab someone with one and then it melts, so there's no murder weapon to help the police solve the murder."

"But the video showed no one close enough to stab him."

"He could have been stabbed a few seconds before the tourist started videoing. He feels a sudden pain, staggers a few paces trying to stay upright, and when the video begins, he's six feet away from his attacker. So the video shows him falling but not being stabbed. And by the time the police show up, the icicle has melted. Remember it was a warm day for January."

"That sounds unlikely. And anyway, the wound was small. I saw it."

"Icicles can be thin, Hubie. And strong enough to puncture someone if they are frozen really hard."

"Okay, but the real problem with that explanation is there's no way to prove it."

"No," she corrected. "The weapon is gone, but that doesn't mean the stabber is in the clear. Maybe someone saw him making an icicle or carrying one. And if someone saw him carrying an icicle, it's not something they'd forget. We should tell Whit about it."

Before we left, I asked Martin if he knew whether Edith Warner and Tilano had children

"Many people have asked that question. Why you asking now?"

"Sharice had a patient who told her Edith Warner was his grandmother."

"If he'd been talking to me instead of Sharice, he might have said that Edith Warner was his *Tay-tay*. It means *grandmother*, but it's also a term of endearment for any older woman you are close to. Calling her *Tay-tay* doesn't mean they were blood relatives."

Chapter 11

I walked to the police department the next morning, asked to see Detective Fletcher, and was told to take a seat and wait. I was happy to have all the cops around the lobby because two of the guys in shabby clothes looked dangerous. So much so that I wondered why they weren't handcuffed. They were staring at me maliciously.

I was relieved when Whit showed up and took me back to his office where I told him about the icicle theory.

"You musta got that from the Inchaustigui girl. She reads murder mysteries and is always coming up with whacky theories about local murders. I told you no one was close enough to stab him with anything, icicle included."

"But what if he was stabbed before the video started and the stabber had moved away and was one of those people you saw in the video? Gurney Guy takes a few steps wondering if he slipped a disk, and then the tourist starts the video that shows Gurney Guy still upright before he takes a couple of wobbly steps and falls over. And by the time the ambulance and police got there, the icicle had melted."

"Who the hell is Gurney Guy?"

"That's what we've been calling the dead guy. Susannah thought it was disrespectful to keep calling him 'the dead guy'."

"First time she's ever said something makes sense to me, although I don't see as how Gurney Guy is all that respectful."

"So you think she may be onto something?"

"I'll tell you what I think. I think one of them drones flew up behind him and stabbed him with a retractable shill then flew away. Now come around here and take a look at this video the tourist shot."

It was exactly as Whit had described to me. The camera – actually a phone in this case – was panning the Plaza. Gurney Guy was walking more or less towards the camera. The three other people in view were a guy to his left, a guy to his right, and a woman behind him, all of them way too far away to stab him. The camera is panning left to right. Just as Gurney Guy is about to go out of the frame, he grimaces and takes an awkward step. The tourist must have noticed it and returned the camera's aim to Gurney Guy, who takes two small steps then begins to stumble. The tourist hits the zoom function and I can see Gurney Guy's face just before he hits the ground.

"See anything I mighta missed?" Whit asks.

"No. I think my untended injury theory might be right."

Whit grabbed his coat and said, "I got to meet a couple of guys in the lobby."

"Be careful; they look dangerous. They were staring at me"

"They are dangerous. To criminals. They're undercover cops, Hubert."

~

My next stop was the University where I entered the outer office of Dean Gangji. A cheerful woman smiled at me and said. "Good morning, Mr. Schuze. My name is Jane Robinson, Dean Gangji's administrative assistant. I am so happy you came by because I have a great deal of paperwork for you. Do you have time to deal with it now?"

I told her I did, wondering how she knew who I was.

She picked up a thick manila folder and led me into the room where I had been railroaded into the position of interim department head.

I declined her offer of coffee. Several hours later I was wishing she had offered lunch.

The first piece of paperwork was an employment application.

I smiled at her and said, "I guess I need to tell you that Dean Gangji already offered me the job on Wednesday, and I accepted it."

"Yes. He was so happy you agreed to serve. So now all you have to do is fill out an application."

"So even though I never applied for the job and I already have it, I have to fill out an application?"

"Exactly," she said, evidently pleased that I caught on so fast.

Next came retirement forms. I had an option between The Educational Retirement Board defined-benefit plan and the Alternative defined-contribution plan. I chose the latter because it was listed first and the form to enroll in it was shorter.

Then came paperwork for health benefits, vision benefits, dental benefits, and disability benefits. I turned them all down.

"You don't want health insurance?"

"I'm healthy," I said.

The employee contribution was $200 a month. I had the job for 5 months, so I'd have to pay a thousand dollars. And likely not get a dime paid for my health care because the deductible was $1500. By the time I spent that much on health care, I'd no longer be employed at UNM.

Next I had to read and sign forms acknowledging that I read and understood policies dealing with nepotism, conflicts of interest, hazardous materials, student privacy, use and care of university equipment under my jurisdiction, affirmative action, equal educational opportunity, campus emergency plans, sick leave, vacation leave, family leave, stewardship of documents, and of course, most importantly, the parking regulations.

Then there was a form granting permission for the University to do a background check. I have been arrested several times, charged with murder which never stuck more than a few hours, and have violated the Archaeological Resources Protection Act hundreds of times. Charges don't count. And I've never been caught digging for ancient pottery.

Still, the idea of a background check was a bit unnerving, especially in light of all the pictures of me that I never knew existed until Charles Webbe enlightened me about widespread surveillance.

It was after three when Ms. Robinson gave me my handbook for department heads, a "stats and data" folder, the minutes of the department head meetings for the previous semester (to bring me up to speed, she explained) and a master key to the Art Building.

Then she gave me the Holy Grail. A sticker for the Bronco which entitled me to park in the space reserved for the head of the art department.

~

The main door to the Art Building is open. I walk to the department head's office and try the knob. It's locked. The key slides in easily. I crack the door open with trepidation. And my right hand.

Of course the blood has been cleaned off the wall behind the desk. The desk chair is new. The old one probably broke when both Milton Shorter and it were propelled backwards by the shot that killed him. Or maybe it was blood-stained and harder to clean than a wall. Everything else is just as I remember it, including the aircraft carrier of a desk.

It's just a place, I tell myself. *It has nothing to do with what happened in it.*

Then I remember a passage from *The House at Otowi Bridge:*

~

> During the centuries of the Crusades in Europe, the time of the great khans in Asia, through the days when Columbus struggled for ships and money to sail west to the Orient, Indians were living in settled communities among these canyons and mesas. When the Spaniards came in the sixteenth century they found the villages deserted. The dwellings had fallen into mounds of stone. The sacred kivas were open to the sun and rain. No one knew what had become of the ancient inhabitants. Perhaps drought drove them away. Perhaps they felt their gods

had failed them, or that they had failed their gods. Some of the Indians living along the Rio Grande claim them as their ancestors, but no one has been able to make the broken pieces of the puzzle fit together. A few years ago, returning for a nostalgic visit to scenes of my own childhood, I slept for a night on the ground below Tsirege, one of the largest of the ancient villages. The word means Place of the Bird People. Carried over into Spanish as *Pajarito,* "little bird," it became the name by which the whole plateau is known. Long ago, for two magic years, my restless father managed a dude-ranch in Pajarito Canyon, two miles above the now-forbidding fence. When I was a child of twelve, I used to ride my barebacked horse to Tsirege and spend hours wondering about the vanished people who had chosen to build their homes in situations of such extraordinary beauty. I remember nothing so still as the silence around that mesa.

~

I know exactly how she felt alone atop that mesa. There is nothing so quiet as a desert at night, especially when a human presence keeps the nocturnal denizens in the shadows. The people who made the pots I dig for are also there, hidden by time rather than shadow. They inhabited this land before Europe knew it existed. Cynics would call it a rationalization, but I think they want me to find their pots, to bring their creations back to the world of the living.

Milton Shorter is not in this office the way the Bird People were on that mesa for Peggy Pond Church or the Anasazi potters are in the desert for me. Maybe because Shorter, even though now deceased, belongs to the present. Maybe because it was just an office, not a home, much less a village.

I didn't know if I would be able to use this office, didn't know how strong the flashbacks might be. I sit on the new chair. Then I stand and adjust it upwards so that I can actually get my arms on the desktop.

I open the "stats and data" folder and begin to study it. And eventually realize that my belief that I'm totally unqualified to be department head is wrong. I abandoned my math major because everyone told me there were no jobs for people with a B.S. in math. I switched to accounting and worked as an accountant for a few years until the boredom got to me. The people who advised me to study accounting were well-intentioned. They assumed accounting is like math.

It isn't. Accounting is not about numbers. It is about rules, categories, and procedures. And all the material in the manila folders looks like accounting. The only difference is the things being manipulated are not debits, credits, profits and losses. They are enrollment numbers, class sizes, grade point averages, and room schedules.

I might be able to do this.

Chapter 12

Sharice turned from the kitchen counter where she was chopping something and said, "I thought you'd be back early."

"So did I. But it took most of the day to do the paperwork."

"Did you go to your new office?"

"Yes."

"And?"

"A bit eerie, but not as bad as I anticipated. I think I can work in it. What are you preparing?"

"Something for both of us, *Quebecois* and New Mexican. I'm calling it *Poutine de yucca*."

"Which is?"

"I'll tell you later."

"Okay, shall I pour the Gruet?"

"Let's wait for Charles. He called and asked if he could come by this evening, and I said yes. Hope you don't mind."

"Not at all. Maybe he'll tell me why he wanted a DNA sample."

Benz' ears twitched, and he walked to the door just before the bell rang. I opened the door and told Charles our cat knew he was outside the door.

"Yeah, I heard his claws tapping the concrete floor," he said.

I didn't know whether he was kidding. Charles Webbe is the most alert human I've even been around.

Sharice filled three coupes and placed a bowl of candied pecans on the coffee table.

After a bit of small talk, Charles got to the purpose of his visit. "The bureau doesn't investigate murders unless they are linked to interstate crime or involve federal matters such as sedition or hate crimes. Since we don't know the identity of the person murdered in the Old Town Plaza, there's no reason for us to be involved at this point. But we are informally assisting the Albuquerque Police Department by using our facial recognition software. Do you know about that technology?"

"The most recent technology I'm aware of is the wheel."

He laughed and said, "That must be a potter's joke. Facial recognition is a method of recognizing a human face. A facial recognition system creates a geometric map of your face from a photograph or video. It stores that map and then when shown another picture of you, it knows it's you."

"Humans are already pretty good at recognizing faces. Why do we need computers to do it?"

"Because although humans see thousands of faces every month, they don't remember most of them. And even the ones they do remember, they usually can't identify. So you see a guy with widely-spaced eyes and a turned up nose. I show you a picture of him later, and you say, 'Yeah, I saw him walking down the street'. Doesn't help me much. But I show that picture to our software and it pulls up other pictures of him. And in many cases, it has a name to go with the face."

Sharice frowned and asked how that was possible.

"Well, one example is if you've ever flown, we have your name and picture in the system."

"They take pictures of everyone going through the security check?" she guessed.

"Video actually. And because they also have your names in the order you entered – remember you have to show your ID and boarding pass – they can pair every face with a name."

"And I'm guessing the same could be said of anyone who's ever gone into a bank," I said, remembering the picture of me in mine.

He nodded.

"What if the bank cared about the privacy of its customers and didn't want to do that?" Sharice asked.

"It's called the FDIC. No bank can operate without its approval, and all banks have to follow its rules."

"Sounds like Orwell's *1984*."

"Except in that story it was Big Brother – the government. Today the private uses of facial recognition software are even larger than what the government does."

"Private companies can do that?"

"Can and do. Aggressively. Apple uses facial recognition to unlock its iPhone X and XS. Some colleges use facial recognition software to take roll in classes. Facebook uses it when you upload a photo to its platform. They ask if you want to tag people in your photos. If you say yes, it creates a link to their profiles. And here's the one I love – churches have used facial recognition to scan their congregations to see who is attending."

Sharice said, "You have got to be kidding. Churches spy on their own members?"

"Guess they just want to know who the true believers are," Charles said.

To which I replied, "Being in church doesn't make you a true believer any more than being in a garage makes you an automobile."

Sharice asked him if every person's face is unique like his or her fingerprints.

"Almost. Facial recognition software can't distinguish identical twins, but other than that, it is amazingly accurate. But not completely. Just like any software, it's only as good as the info you feed into it. So, for example, it may not correctly match a blurred photograph or one taken from a strange angle, but it's getting better and better and use of the technology is exploding. The Bureau has over five hundred million individuals in our facial recognition software."

"That's more than the U.S. population."

"Yes. And we have good reason to track people other than citizens."

While Charles and Sharice were discussing the millions of facial images, I was thinking about the two he had of me. "So I'm obviously in the system. But how did that lead to a request for my DNA."

He hesitated for a few seconds then said, "When we ran the picture of the victim through our software, it spit back pictures of you."

I heard Sharice's sudden intake of air and saw her turn to face me.

I said, "The facial recognition thought it was me?"

"No. It had no exact matches, so it gave us the closest ones."

"And?"

He hesitated a moment before speaking. "You and he are close relatives."

No wonder he looked familiar, I thought to myself. *But if we look so alike, why didn't I notice?* After a few moments thinking about it, I thought I had an explanation. Then I said to

Charles, "You say facial recognition is not perfect. How about DNA comparisons."

"Virtually foolproof. I suppose a technician might accidentally mislabel a sample, but short of that, if a DNA comparison shows two people are close relatives, then they are."

"Define close."

"The lab woman who ran the test said you and the victim share about twenty-five percent of your DNA. So genetically, the victim would have to be one of your grandparents, an aunt or uncle, a niece or nephew, or a partial sibling."

"How old is he?" I asked.

"Won't know until we ID him. You saw him. How old would you guess he is?"

"I glanced at him for about five seconds, and I wasn't trying to determine his age, but he certainly wasn't old enough to be one of my grandparents. Maybe around my age or younger. He's not an aunt or niece because he's male. And I'm an only child, so Gurney Guy is not my sibling, partial or otherwise."

Sharice said, "Gurney Guy?"

"Susannah thought it was disrespectful to keep calling him the dead guy, so Martin dubbed him Gurney Guy."

She looked at Charles and said, "They'd probably had several Margaritas."

Charles smiled and said, "Tell me about your family tree."

"Like me, my father was also an only child, so Gurney Guy can't be from his side of the family. My mother had one sister who had one daughter who had one son. You've met Tristan. He calls me his uncle and I call him my nephew, but technically, he is my first cousin once removed. But he is alive and well. So there has to be a mistake in the DNA test."

Charles shook his head. "Not necessarily."

Then he was silent for a moment.

Sharice moved closer to me and took my hand.

Charles said, "There are other possibilities, scenarios you will dislike. So keep in mind that I'm not suggesting that any of these scenarios are factual."

I nodded and he proceeded. "Either of your parents could have had a child you didn't know about. If your mother had a child, she might have put the child up for adoption. If such a thing did happen, then obviously she decided it was better for you not to know about it. It may be that your father also didn't know about it. Or perhaps your father got a woman pregnant at some point. The bottom line is you may have a partial sibling you never knew."

"I hope I don't have a partial sibling."

"It's only a possibility," Charles reminded me.

"How do we find out for sure?"

"We put the Bureau on it," he said and flashed a big smile. "We're pretty good at finding things out."

"How would you discover whether I have an unknown sibling?"

"Legwork. We'd do complete background checks on your parents, talk to everyone we can find who knew them, worked with them, etc. We'd examine birth records in the time span when your parents were of child-bearing age. It's slow and methodical. But it usually works."

I ate a few sugared pecans and took a sip of my Gruet. Did I want the FBI snooping around in my parents' pasts? Did I have any right to object? After all, if the FBI is the pot of snoopers, then I'm the black kettle. I unearth personal property of people long dead. And unlike the FBI, my snooping is not condoned by statute.

But the people in whose past I intrude are nameless. They have no reputation to worry about, much less records of anything in their life. Except what they made. It's all that is left of them. They want me to find it so that at least we know they lived and made things of beauty.

Today everyone has a birth certificate, a Social Security card, and eventually a death certificate. Maybe after they get that last one, we should leave them alone.

"What would be the point of finding out how I'm related to Gurney Guy?"

"From your point of view or from law enforcement's point of view?"

"Start with law enforcement."

"Knowing who he is makes it a lot easier to find out who killed him. Unsolved murders make cops cranky."

"Are there other ways to discover who he is?"

"Yes, and the Albuquerque Police are pursuing those as we speak. Checking all the missing person reports, showing his picture to retailers who sell Ermenegildo Zegna suits and Salvatore Ferragamo shoes, things like that."

"Will that work?"

"Don't know."

Sharice asked me if I even wanted to know about the victim. She didn't call him Gurney Guy.

"I don't know if I do or not. And even if I decide I would like to know more about him, I'm not sure that would be enough to justify prying into any secrets my parents may have had."

"We won't do any background work on your parents without your consent," said Charles. "If it were an FBI matter, that would be different. But at this point it's a simple homicide and therefore a matter for the Albuquerque Police Department. And they lack the manpower, the expertise and the desire to do any background checks on your parents."

"So how will they solve the murder?" Sharice asked.

"They might get lucky and get a tip. Or they might find something in the body that connects to a weapon, a small piece of it or a trace chemical connected to its manufacture, use, or cleaning."

Sharice piped up, "How about dental work? You could show his x-rays around to all the dental offices."

Charles chuckled and said, "We could deputize you to do that, but he never had any dental work. No implants, no bridges, not even a filling."

"Wow. About 92% of all Americans have fillings. He must have had a great dental hygienist," she said.

Chapter 13

Turns out that *poutine* is a popular Canadian snack of French fries covered with cheese curds and brown gravy.

I have no idea what curds looks like and have never heard the word spoken except when it precedes *and whey*.

Sharice substituted yucca for the potatoes, *cotija* cheese for the curds and tomatillo salsa for the gravy. The yucca fries were light and crisp, the cotija pleasingly granular and salty and the tomatillo salsa tart and spicy. And the dish was perfect with chilled Gruet *Blanc de Noir*.

But then what isn't?

Sharice said, "I'm surprised you enjoyed the meal so much after hearing Charles' bombshell."

"Can't let a little thing like finding out you may have a brother that you saw only after he was dead spoil your appetite."

She stared at me. "You don't believe that, do you?"

"I do. I'm a strong believer in not letting my appetite be spoiled."

She jabbed me in the ribs and said, "You know what I mean."

"I do, and you're right. I don't believe Gurney Guy is my brother."

"You think they made a mistake with the DNA?"

"No. He looked like me, so we may be related. But he is not my brother because the timing doesn't work. My parents had me later in life than usual. My mother was in her early forties and my father even older. Like most couples, they wanted children. But it took a long time to happen. And there wasn't much they could do about it. Remember I was born in 1969 before various fertility methods became popular. My parents had probably given up hope. But fortunately for me, they hadn't given up sex. Since I was a surprise baby, I can't imagine my mother had a child before me. And if my father had a child with another woman before he met my mother, both my mother and I would have known about it. He was a stand-up guy; he would not have kept that secret from us."

"So who is ... I don't want to call him Gurney Guy; its sounds flippant."

"Then call him Floss Man. He had to be a diligent flosser to make it to forty or fifty or whatever age he was without a single cavity."

"Okay. So who is Floss Man?"

"Well, one reason I didn't freak out as much as I normally would is that I started thinking about who might be that close to me kinship-wise as soon as Charles said Floss Man and I are related. And the only possibility is that Floss Man is Tristan's half-brother."

"Why?"

"Did I never tell you about his weird grandmother and mother?"

"No."

"Well his grandmother was my mother's sister, which is hard to believe because no two women have ever been more different from one another. My mother was contained and organized. Bea, on the other hand, was a flower child. Maybe it's just all this talk about my family tree, which is actually more of a bush because it's so small, but it dawns on me that maybe my aunt Beatrice was one of those babies that got switched in the hospital nursery."

"Being a flower child was common for women in her generation. Was she weird in some other way?"

"She named her daughter after her."

"Men do that all the time with their sons. I think it's cool that she did that with her daughter."

"Do you think it's cool that she called her daughter 'Junior'?"

"Hey, if she wanted to co-opt that male naming system, why not go all the way?"

"Okay, let's move on to Junior. She eloped with a guitar player named Rhino who was playing a one-night gig in Tucumcari."

"Love at first sight is so romantic."

"He brought her back to Tucumcari eight months after they left, and they had Tristan exactly one month later."

"Her first night away from home must have been something special."

"Rhino was so happy about Tristan that he got drunk and died in a one-car crash."

"Poor Junior. And poor Tristan."

"I have to admit that although Junior's weird, she did a great job raising Tristan."

"Yes, he is a son any mother would be proud of. But how does this relate to Floss Man?"

I liked Gurney Guy better than Floss Man, but I didn't tell her that. "It's possible that Rhino was not Junior's first rodeo."

"So you think Junior had Floss Man before she met Rhino?"

"Exactly. But just because I managed to take the startling news and remain calm, doesn't mean I might not begin to freak out."

"Why?"

"Because the news that Floss Man is related to me explains why he looked familiar. But it unexplains somethings else."

"*Unexplains* is not a word."

"It should be because this is the perfect time to use it. Whit showed me the paper Floss Man had with my name and the address of my shop on it. The explanation was he was going to my shop to buy a pot. But now that theory has been unexplained. And I don't much like the new theory."

She figured it out quickly. "He was coming to tell you he is a cousin you didn't know about."

"Yeah. And the next question is why he wanted to tell me after all these years."

"Maybe he just found out about it himself?"

"Possibly. And if that was the case, is his murder somehow related?"

"You don't know he was murdered."

So I repeated the story of the tourist's video happening to show the dead guy fall over. She suggested he was shot, and I told her why that had been ruled out and the other various theories that had been put forward, including the icicle theory which she laughed at.

"You going to be alright?"

"Yeah. I'm hoping the wound was an accident that he didn't realize was potentially fatal and just didn't get it tended to properly."

But I was thinking a guy that fastidious wouldn't have left a wound unattended.

Sharice said, "I think there's a problem with your theory that Floss Man is Tristan's half-brother. Tristan looks nothing like you. He has a bigger frame and dark curly hair. None of his features – ears, eyes, nose – look like yours. But

Floss Man looked so much like you that the facial recognition popped up photos of you."

"Phenotype and genotype," I replied. "Tristan has genes from both Junior and Rhino, but the Rhino ones ended up dominant. But in her first son – Floss Man – her genes were dominant."

"Or Beatrice was in fact switched in the nursery, and the reason Tristan doesn't look like you is he's not related to you."

I had been joking, of course, but now I realized I might have accidentally hit a hidden truth. One I didn't like.

I felt a bit better when Sharice asked if Junior looks like me. I'd never thought about it. I hadn't seen her in years, and I'd never had reason to examine her looks in comparison to mine.

"I'll let you be the judge of whether Junior looks like me. And I'm sure she has a picture of her mother, so you can see whether I look like my aunt Bea," I said. "How would you like a short vacation in Tucumcari next weekend?"

"Sounds good. I've never been there. But one final question about Floss Man. If he looks so much like you that facial recognition software popped up photos of you, why didn't you notice the similarity?"

"I did. Remember I told you he looked familiar?"

"Familiar is one thing. Looking like a twin brother is another."

"Twin brother is too strong. But I thought about it while Charles was here, and I think I know the reason why I missed how strong the resemblance is. Three reasons actually. First, I looked at him for about five seconds. Second, my instruction from Whit was to see if I could ID him, not to see if he looked like me. And third – and most important – people look a lot different when they're dead. The thing we notice most about people is their countenance, which is not their face. It's their expression. When I look at you, I see your bright smile and intelligent eyes. When I look at Susannah, I see her naiveté and unbounded enthusiasm. Dead people don't have expressions. So they don't look much like themselves. Facial recognition software focuses on your face's geometry. Humans focus on your countenance."

Chapter 14

The Central New Mexico Correctional Facility is located in Los Lunas. It has a maximum capacity of 666 offenders.

I did not make up that number, and I can't help wondering if the designer picked it as a statement of some sort.

I avoided Interstate 25 by driving south on Broadway. With its junkyards, cement plants, small refinery, welding shops, feedstores and rock piles, it's hardly the scenic route, but anything beats the high-speed monotony of a freeway. Broadway becomes NM highway 47 and hugs the east bank of the Rio Grande, passing through the Isleta Pueblo, Bosque Farms and Heritage Park where I turned west onto NM 6 and crossed the river into Los Lunas.

The prison is on the south end of the town nestled up against I-25. The entrance is on Morris Road. Except on this day, I suppose Frederick Blass saw it as the exit.

He was already a free man, wearing a normal grey suit that looked to be two sizes too large, standing just outside the gate next to a corrections officer, the two of them chatting casually like old friends.

When Freddie released me from the hug

he'd greeted me with, he was crying.

The corrections officer looked at me and said, "We're going to miss this man. He did more good inside than any employee ever did."

I introduced myself to the officer – his name was Jaime Delatorre – and he asked me for my drivers license. I showed it to him and he handed me a clipboard and asked me to read the paper on it and sign it at the bottom.

I did as he directed and asked, "Just out of curiosity, why did I have to read and sign that."

He smiled and said, "If you didn't sign, we'd still let Freddie go, but we'd put you in his cell."

Good to know that some prison workers still have a sense of humor.

"Actually, Freddie was free once he passed through that gate. He could have just walked away. But it sort of spooks the locals to see former prisoners strolling through town, so we prefer to have someone meet the discharged person. And we also care about our people, so we want a record of who they left with."

Delatorre gave Freddie a bear hug and watched us drive away.

As we drove down Morris Street, I asked Freddie where he wanted to go.

"Frontier," he said, referring to Albuquerque's most popular eatery. It was established when I was two years old, so from my point of view, it's always been there. Directly across the street from UNM, it serves about 4000 meals a day. My parents often ate there with me when I was a kid. It was cheap, good, and only about 600 yards from our house on Dartmouth. When I became a college student, I moved a few blocks into a dorm because my parents thought I should have a 'true college experience'.

Or maybe they just wanted me out of the house.

Packed with noisy students, Frontier was more of a true college experience than the dorm, which was merely a place to sleep.

I reversed my route to get to Albuquerque. When we reached Bosque Farms, Freddie asked me to pull over. He got out and walked into an apple orchard. Sensing he wanted to be alone, I stayed in the Bronco. It was in the fifties but there was no wind and the sun's rays flooded through the dry desert air. After a few minutes walking between the trees, Freddie threw his jacket over a low limb, removed his shoes and socks, and began jogging between the trees. After ten minutes he dropped to the ground and rolled around in the yellowed dry grass. Then he stilled and stared up at the trees.

After a few minutes, I suspected he may have fallen asleep, but he got up, walked back to the Bronco and said, "Home, James."

"Where is home?"

"Good question. A real estate agent sold the condo at Rio Grande Lofts for me, so I am officially homeless. Which sounds good compared to my recent digs."

"I guess buying back your place in Rio Grande Lofts is out of the question?"

"Definitely." He smiled and added, "You broke into the place several times. I want something more secure."

I laughed and asked, "Where will you stay during your house hunt?"

"A cheap motel."

"I've got a better idea. You can stay for free in my little residence at the back of my shop while you look for a place of your own."

"As I recall, your place has one bed, and it's a single."

"Yep, probably about like your cell. Except you can come and go as you please."

"Where will you sleep?"

"I live in a condo on Silver."

He swiveled to look at me. "One of those glass and steel places?"

"Yep."

"I had you pegged as an adobe guy."

"I am. But my girlfriend is not. She owns the condo."

The silence that followed was so awkward, it almost tripped on its shoelaces.

He looked away from me out the passenger window and asked, "Anyone I know?"

"It's not Susannah."

"Sorry. You told me that when you visited last year. But I remembered the way you two were together. You were lovers and didn't know it."

I didn't want to 'go there' as they say these days, so I said, "Her name is Sharice. She was my dental hygienist. Now she's my live-in girlfriend. More accurately, I'm her live-in boyfriend since it's her condo."

"You still run Spirits in Clay?"

"No. I still own it, but an Englishman named Gladwyn Farthing minds the store for me. He also rents the space which I own next to Spirits in Clay. He has a desert outdoor clothing and supply store there and minds both shops."

"He doesn't use the residence in the back of yours?"

"No. He lives in the third unit of the building, the one on the opposite end from Spirits in Clay."

"I thought Miss Gladys owned that one."

"She does. She and Gladwyn married last year so he lives in her place."

He was silent for a few minutes. "Nothing much changes inside. Same cell, same meals, same guards. And mostly the same fellow inmates since it's not exactly short-term lodging.

And you figure out quickly that keeping up with the outside world only reinforces the reality that you aren't in it. So you stop thinking of anything except day-to-day routine and whatever habit or hobby you can engage in or invent. Like the birdman of Alcatraz who tamed wild birds that came to the ledge of his cell window."

"In your case it was teaching painting."

"Best thing I ever did. Like I told you when you visited, some of the students I taught at UNM had talent, but they hadn't lived enough to put any soul into their work. In prison, I taught guys who had always been losers, always done the wrong thing. And they found out by painting that they could do something creative rather than destructive."

"And did you also paint?"

"I did. If I had eight students, I'd set up nine easels, and we'd all paint. Of course I started them out making copies. I'd make periodic rounds to give them pointers and encouragement. After a while, they started doing the same for me, laughing as they tried to critique my work and happy when I sometimes took their advice."

"What artists did you select to copy?"

"Renoir, Cezanne, Manet, anyone who paints with feeling. The guys wanted to make up their own compositions, but I told them you start by copying. Once you get the hang of it, you can do your own thing."

"Harte Hockley told me that when his students ask why he requires them to make precise copies of paintings by artists like Cezanne, he tells them, 'If you can't copy, you can't paint'. Copying is how we develop the eye'."

"He's a huge talent. I'll never be that good a painter. But I also know I can teach it."

I had turned right from Broadway onto Central and we were at the western edge of the campus when Freddie said, "We'll never get a parking space."

I turned into the campus and parked in my private space.

"You can't park here." he said, "This spot is reserved."

I smiled and said, "You sure?"

"Of course I'm sure. I parked in this spot for years. It's reserved for the head of the art department."

I pointed to the sticker on my windshield and said, "That would be me."

Chapter 15

I convinced Freddie to hold his barrage of questions until after we ordered and were seated, which at Frontier are two distinct operations.

He spotted a couple leaving a table and grabbed it while telling me he wanted the Frontier burrito – beef, beans, and green chile inside with green chile stew & cheese on top. I chose the chicken enchiladas. The ordering line moved fast because there were several cashiers taking orders. I was back at the table in under five minutes, but that was long enough for Freddie to have calmed down a bit.

I don't like the term 'bus boy' and wouldn't have applied it to the guy cleaning our table even if I did because he looked to be in his seventies. But by whatever title, I admired his speed and dedication. The look on his face said, *I am proud to do my job well.* He chatted with us as he worked and wished us a good day when he left.

In addition to feeding thousands of people a day and being a landmark of Albuquerque, this crazy eating establishment in a barn employs scores of semi-skilled workers who might otherwise be forced to be on public assistance.

And the cooks, cashiers, table cleaners and all the other workers have the hustle and good cheer of a team.

I suppose it is possible to eat a Frontier burrito with your hands, but it is not advisable. Freddie cut off a bite with his knife, lifted it to his mouth with his fork, and closed his eyes as he chewed.

"Better than where you've been eating?" I asked. I almost said *better than prison food* but caught myself in time.

He was still chewing, so he just nodded. After he swallowed, he said, "The food there wasn't bad. Just monotonous. So if you're now the department head, obviously Milton Shorter is back to teaching metals or art therapy or whatever he happens to be into at this point. How did they finally remove him as department head? He had already set a record as the longest serving interim in history."

The question brought home to me full force the degree to which prison yanks people out of the normal world. There were newspapers in the prison library and a television in a rec room, but Freddie never read the former or watched the latter. It made me realize his statement that he didn't keep up with the outside world while in prison was true. He didn't even know Shorter was dead.

"Milton was murdered last month."

"Oh my god. How did that happen?"

So here it goes again, me having to recount the murder of Milton Shorter. Freddie was finally free. But I was still captive. And unlike Freddie when he'd been inside, I had no scheduled release date. I told myself to stop this self-pity, but my self was only paying partial attention to me.

"He was shot to death in his office as a result of a family dispute."

He shook his head slowly. "Unbelievable. So how did you become head? When you visited me, you told me you were an adjunct teaching one course."

I sighed. "It's a long story."

He smiled and said, "I learned patience during my long vacation at taxpayer expense."

I told him about my students deciding they would each enter a pot in the student/faculty art show. Told him how diligently they'd worked on their projects, and that even though some of their pieces were excellent, they were all rejected.

"Departmental politics," he said.

"Right. So they decided to stage their own show in the hall outside the gallery."

"A *salon des refusés*. Brilliant!"

"And successful. So much so that Junior Prather went bonkers and attacked me. He was convicted of felony assault and dismissed from the university. So the department was lacking a ceramicist, and Dean Gangji made me a full-time temp. Which made me technically eligible to serve as interim head. The faculty elected me because the only other person who was willing to take the job was Melvin Armstrong."

I sat back in my chair, satisfied with my succinct summary that explained how I became interim department head and did not reveal any of the complicated and gruesome details.

My satisfaction evaporated when Freddie said, "But I explained to you last fall that there was not enough demand for ceramics classes to justify two positions. Junior being dismissed was a perfect opportunity to reduce the ceramics faculty to one person and use the money from Junior's position to hire a full-time and day-time digital art teacher because that's what the students want today."

So much for simple. "Well, the need to replace Junior was what the dean used as an excuse when he made me a full-time temp. But it turned out that the real reason was he needed me to be eligible to serve as head because no one else would do it, and he didn't want Armstrong."

Freddie shook his head and said, "I'd forgotten how bizarre the academic world is. Makes prison seem almost normal. Do you have any idea how to be a department head?"

"Susannah asked me that same—"

"Sorry to interrupt, but I withdraw the question. It's presumptuous of me to ask since I don't know how to do it even though I had the job for a number of years."

"According to some people, you did it fairly well. And I hope they're right."

"Why?"

"Because I plan to be Charlie McCarthy to your Edgar Bergen. When anyone asks me a question or wants me to make some sort of choice, I'll tell them I need to consider it. Then you'll advise me of the best thing to do, and I'll present it as if I thought of it."

"I'm not sure you should put that much trust in me."

"It's not a matter of trust. I have no place else to turn. You're the only department head I know. And on top of that, I need to get some compensation for allowing you to live free in Spirits in Clay."

"So being the shadow chairman is my rent?"

"Exactly."

After he managed to eat the entire Frontier burrito, I asked him what he wanted next.

"The three things I missed most in prison were freedom, sex, and booze."

"In that order?"

"Yes."

"Rock and Roll didn't make the list."

"No."

"Well you have your freedom. I can't do anything about the sex part, but I will buy you a drink."

You will not be surprised to learn that I took him to *Dos Hermanas*.

Chapter 16

Angie swirled up to our table, her colorful *folklorico* skirt fanning her lemony perfume through the masa-scented air.

"A margarita with salt for you and," she turned to Freddie, "what are you having, handsome?"

He smiled and answered, "What do you recommend?"

"Got to know a bit about you to make a recommendation. You local?"

"From Colorado, but lived most of my life in Albuquerque."

"*¿Hablas español?*"

"*Un poco.*"

"Had anything recently you liked?"

"The last drink I had was over six years ago."

"Uh-oh. You been in the 12-step program?"

He laughed. "Nope. I've been in prison."

She also laughed. "You're joking."

He shook his head. "I was released today. Hubie picked me up down in Los Lunas and took me to Frontier for a late lunch and then here for a drink of ... well, whatever you recommend."

She put her hand on his shoulder and said,

"I have just the thing for you."

The drink she returned with was in a margarita glass, but the liquid was darker, as if someone had used tequila *añejo*. There are people who make margaritas with dark aged tequila, but there are also people who make apple pies using Ritz Crackers instead of apples.

"It's called 'freedom'," she said. "Tequila *añejo*, ancho chile liqueur, and lime juice."

"I'll drink to freedom," I said and lifted my glass.

He clinked his glass against mine, took a sip, and pronounced it delicious.

Angie bent down, kissed his forehead, and said, "Welcome back."

He watched her walk away, her long black hair swaying with each step.

"Wow."

"That for the drink or for Angie."

"Both. I've been here a couple of times, once or twice with Susannah and you. Obviously, Angie doesn't remember me."

I was looking slightly to his left as he spoke. Susannah had just entered. She looked at our table, hesitated, then turned and left.

I guess Freddie looked different enough that a casual acquaintance might no longer recognize him. But someone who had slept with him for several months would. And obviously did.

After we finished our drinks – he said he

was limiting himself to one because of the long dry spell – we walked to Miss Gladys' Gift Shop. Inviting Freddie to bunk behind my shop had been spur-of-the-moment, and I didn't want Glad Farthing showing up in the morning to mind Spirits in Clay and discovering a vagrant in my former residence.

I introduced Freddie to Glad. He invited us in and said that Gladys was cooking dinner and he hoped we'd join them.

Before I could fabricate an excuse for declining the invite, Freddie said, "It does smell delicious," and I remembered that even though he knew Miss Gladys, he didn't know her as *Nuestra Señora de los caseroles* as she is affectionately known in Old Town.

The building she and I own parts of is over three hundred years old. Its history began when Juan de Oñate entered what is now New Mexico on July 11, 1598, twenty-two years before the Pilgrims landed at Plymouth Rock and even before Jamestown which most history books mistakenly describe as the first European settlement in what is now the U.S.

Oñate brought 500 Spanish settlers and soldiers and 7,000 head of livestock. They worked their way north along the Rio Grande, some of them settling near what would eventually become Albuquerque. They seized control of the indigenous people, taught them

Spanish, and forcibly converted them to Christianity.

That's what happens when you allow hordes of illegal aliens into your homeland.

The second unwelcome flow of immigrants was from Texas, a trend that continues today. Most of the people who own vacation cabins in New Mexico are Texans wanting to escape the heat and other Texans.

Miss Gladys' husband was a wealthy cotton merchant who moved from Texas to New Mexico on the advice of his doctor. It didn't help. Miss Gladys soon became a widow.

Being a resourceful and energetic woman, she used some of her inheritance to purchase the east third of our ancient adobe in Old Town where she opened the eponymous shop therein. When I purchased the west third of the building, we became neighbors and friends, and I became the recipient of casserole leftovers. Her official excuse was that all her recipes were for casseroles for two. In fact, it would have been easy to make smaller casseroles since all the ingredients are easily halved; e.g., one can of Campbell's Cream of Chicken Soup instead of two, one bag of Kraft shredded cheddar instead of two, etc.

As you have no doubt figured out, her real motivation was to feed the poor guy who didn't have a wife and to once again have someone to cook for.

The frequency of casserole deliveries lessened considerable after she and Gladwyn married. There are seldom any leftovers now. Glad actually loves the casseroles. Having grown up in England, he probably thinks of them as *haute cuisine.*

But even he must have been taken aback when Miss Gladys announced we were having Baked Eyeballs Casserole.

Freddie laughed and said, "I had lamb eyeballs once in Morocco. After you get past the idea, it's not bad, sort of like eating very tough hardboiled eggs."

Miss Gladys' hand went to her mouth. "Oh my. You must be a brave man. I can assure you there are no eyeballs in this dish."

She placed the large baking dish on a trivet next to her on the table and instructed us to pass our plates. I knew this to be her method of portion control, which in her case means you get twice as much as you want.

She described the dish as she ladled it onto our plates. "It's as easy as falling off a log. One jar of Prego Italian Sausage & Garlic Italian Sauce, one 15-ounce tub of ricotta cheese, one small bag of Kraft grated Parmesan cheese, one box of bow-tie pasta boiled and drained, one container of fresh mozzarella cheese balls, and one small can of sliced black olives. Just put the pasta in the casserole dish, dump in the sauce and stir it around, spread the ricotta and parmesan, then bake until it's bubbling hot. After it comes out of the oven, line up the mozzarella balls on top of it and place one olive slice on each ball to make them look like eyes."

As usual, it tasted better than it sounded, especially because by the time she ladled it onto the plate, the olive slices had fallen of the mozzarella balls so that the dish wasn't staring me in the face as I ate it.

When Freddie requested a second helping, Miss Gladys said, "I do love to see a man enjoy his food."

"He must really love it," I said. "He ate an entire Frontier burrito at lunch."

"Zounds," said Glad, "the fellow is a true trencherman."

One of Gladwyn's many endearing traits is his colorful phrasing.

"Just trying to get back the weight I've lost over the last six years," said Freddie.

"You poor dear." said Miss Gladys. "Have you been ill?"

"No, I've been in prison."

"Oh, my!"

"He completed his term today," I interjected quickly. I feared Miss Gladys was about to ask the obvious question and didn't know how she might react when told that he'd been in for manslaughter. And I kept talking. "He served his term and wants to put the past behind him. The warden praised him for working to help other prisoners achieve rehabilitation."

"How did he do that?" asked Glad.

"I taught them painting," Freddie responded.

"So they can get jobs painting houses when they are released?"

Freddie laughed and said, "Not that kind of painting, although it might have been better for them if they had learned house painting. I taught them how to paint pictures. I was an art professor at UNM."

"Do I know you?" asked Miss Gladys.

"We met briefly. I'm surprised and honored that you remember me."

"You were introduced this evening as Freddie. But your real name is Frederick. Let me think a moment ... Blass! You are Frederick Blass."

He made a movement best described as a curtsy of the head. "At your service, Miss Gladys."

"And you were convicted of—"

"And served his time," said Glad looking at Miss Gladys, "and is spending his first night as a free man as our guest for dinner."

Her eyes twinkled. "I believe it is time for cake."

Chapter 17

I was pulling into my reserved parking space on the first day of classes for the spring semester when a thought came to me – no one had assigned me to teach any classes.

A second thought came to me – classes are assigned by the department head.

The third thing wasn't a thought. It was just a feeling – embarrassment.

I made a U-turn and drove to Spirits in Clay where I found Freddie in the shop standing in front of an easel.

"Hi Hubie. If you're looking for Glad, he came in to mind the shop this morning, but I sent him home. I bought some art supplies yesterday at Artisan and decided that since I was going to be here painting, he might as well have some time off. Hope you don't mind."

"I don't mind. How did you get to Artisan? It's over by the University."

"I walked. Every step was a breath of freedom."

"Nice. But it's still a long way."

"Okay, I admit it. They all know me there, so I got a ride back."

"How did you pay for the supplies?"

"Saved my prison wages."

"I have my first question for you as the shadow department head. I'm supposed to be a full-time temp, but I forgot to assign myself any classes and school starts today. Is it too late? And if so, what will happen? And if it's not too late, how do I assign myself classes?"

"Being department head is considered full-time. You don't have to teach. Many department heads teach a course once or twice a year because they enjoy it. But new department heads are way too busy to teach a class."

"So I won't get in trouble?"

"Didn't Dean Gangji talk to you about release time?"

"He said I would teach 4 courses unless I was granted release time for other duties. But I didn't ask what that meant because I didn't think I'd have other duties. And when I did the paperwork with Ms. Robinson, she didn't say anything about it either."

"The release time for department heads is four courses. So you will not be teaching this semester."

"How will I keep busy? How will I earn my pay?"

He laughed and said, "Trust me. After a few days on the job, you won't be worrying about that."

~

I drove back to the university, parked in my

space and entered the art building packed with a line of grumbling students. I excused myself as I went past them and finally arrived at my office only to discover that was where the line began.

"Are you the department head," asked the sullen student at the head of the line.

"I am. Come in."

I unlocked the door, went behind my desk and invited the student to sit down in front of it. I now appreciated the big desk that I had often made fun of; it seemed to be a barrier between me and an angry student.

"I need ART 2000 to graduate, and I can't register for it."

"Let me check." I was happy I'd studied the stats and data folder. I found the page with data about the spring offerings. "There are three sections being offered, and none of them are full. You can register for any one of them."

"No I can't. I also need to register for ART 2100, and it's offered at the same time as ART 2000."

"Well, just take one of the other sections of ART 2000 that doesn't conflict with 2100."

"Have you even looked at the schedule?" he said angrily. "They *all* conflict." The veins in his forehead were showing, and I begin to wonder if the desk was adequate protection.

I looked back at the folder and saw that all three sections of ART 2000 (Basic Design) were indeed offered at the same time, which couldn't be right because they all had Jollo Bakke listed as the instructor, and while she is aggressive, I didn't think she could be in three different places at the same time.

"I apologize for the inconvenience. There seems to be a mistake in the listing of course offerings. This is my first day on the job. I'll get this straightened out."

"You better," he growled and hastily turned to go.

"Would you please ask the next student in line to come in as you leave?" I said to his back.

He nodded.

The young woman who entered was calmer than the first student, but had the same complaint. As did the third student.

I went into the hall and spoke loudly, something I'm not good at. "May I have your attention. The list of course offerings shows all three sections of ART 2000 offered at the same time. That is obviously an error. This is my first day as department head, so it may take a few hours to get this straightened out. But by tomorrow, you should be able to have a choice of three different time slots to choose from. If that is why you are in line, you can leave. If you are here for a different reason, please remain in line."

About half the students dispersed. The other

half had a similar complaint. They couldn't register for ART 3357 Digital Art because all the sections were in the evening. I stood in the hall and explained that the instructor was employed full-time during the day and therefore could teach only in the evening. One young man said. "I have to work to put myself through school. I work as a bartender six evenings a week. I can't give up my job. Why should a university professor get to teach only in the evenings? Let him give up his day job instead of a bunch of us having to give up our night jobs."

"That's a good question," I said, "and the answer bodes well for all of you. His day job pays a lot more than the University does. So if you learn the skills he has, you'll qualify for high-paying positions when you graduate."

"But we won't graduate if we can't take his course."

I thought about it briefly, then said, "As you heard me say to the students who need ART 2000, this is my first day on the job as department head. No one else on the faculty is qualified to teach digital art, and I don't know anybody in town who can teach it. But if any of you know someone who can, let me know, and I'll try to hire him or her to teach a daytime section."

When they all started talking at once, I interrupted them. "Write down names and contact info, and I'll get right on it."

After they handed me the hastily drawn list, I walked to Bakke's office. Her tiny desk faced a window and her back faced the hall. She was bent over the desk with a very small brush in her hand. I knocked on the door frame.

"Go away. I'm busy."

"This will only take a minute."

"The hours when I'm available to students are posted on the door. Come back then."

"I'm not a student."

She whirled around and said, "What do you not understand about … Oh, it's you. What do you want?"

"I need your help to fix a mistake in the class schedule. It shows all three sections of ART 2000 listed at noon on Tuesdays and Thursdays."

"That's not a mistake."

"Then I guess the mistake is listing you as the instructor for all three. Which one are you actually teaching at noon on Tuesdays and Thursdays?"

"All of them."

"You've figured out some way to be in three different places at the same time?" I joked.

She didn't laugh. Nor did she smile. "They're all in the same room."

"I don't understand."

"Then you shouldn't have agreed to serve as

department head. I have neither the time nor the inclination to explain class scheduling to you. As I said, I'm busy." She swung her chair around and went back to whatever she was doing.

I left the building and drove back to Spirits in Clay. Freddie was still painting. I told him about my conversation with Bakke.

"They're called stacked classes," he explained. "It's when two or more classes are taught in the same room at the same time."

"I don't understand how that could work."

"I found it to be useful in certain cases. For example, when I taught Drawing I and Drawing II, I'd schedule them as stacked classes. There were several advantages to doing it that way. Typically, I'd have about ten students in Drawing I and about five in Drawing II. Since the minimum class size is seven, the Drawing II class would have been cancelled by the dean for lack of adequate enrollment. But by stacking the classes, the Drawing II students were able to get a class they wanted. The second advantage was for the Drawing I students who got to see what the more advanced kids were doing. The Drawing II students were like tutors for the Drawing I students. And it helped me because I could teach an extra class without it cutting into my time as department head."

"You said department heads don't have to teach."

"Right, but I wanted to."

"Did you get paid extra for teaching?"

"No. Regular faculty can get overload pay for teaching an extra class, but not department heads."

"Bakke is teaching three sections of ART 2000 as stacked classes. What are the advantages in that case?"

He made a sound somewhere between a laugh and a snort. "It satisfies three-fourths of her teaching load with one class."

"What are the advantages to the students?"

"None. And as you just discovered, the disadvantage is that their ability to schedule is removed, often delaying their graduation and therefore costing them tuition, fees, books, and room and board for another semester."

"Why did you let her do that?"

"I didn't. I guess Shorter must have let her get away with it. Rule 1 for department heads: we exist to help students. Rule 2: many faculty disregard rule 1."

"What should I do?"

"Reschedule two sections of ART 2000 to different times. Bakke will go ballistic. Try to mollify her by letting her pick the hours and days so long as they are all different. Offer her a summer school course that allows her to make a little extra money."

"Will that work?"

"Probably not. But when she files a grievance, you'll have it on record that you tried to work something out in good faith that was fair for both her and the students."

"What if she refuses to teach the course at other times?"

"You already read the handbook. Scheduling is the sole prerogative of the department head. You are required to consult the faculty about their schedule preferences, but the final scheduling decisions are yours."

"I know. And it also says department heads determine who teaches each course, so I suppose I could get someone else to do it, but all the other faculty have full loads."

"You don't have to use them. Think about why you ended up teaching ART 2330 last semester?"

"Armstrong and Prather both refused to do it."

"That's your answer."

"Use an adjunct? Where would I find one?"

"A young woman we both know recently received an M.A. in art. Maybe you should ask her."

~

I drove back to the campus and talked to Bakke as Freddie suggested. And got the result he predicted. She went ballistic and refused to accept any changes in her schedule. I informed her that Section 1 of ART 2000 would remain at noon on Tuesdays and Thursdays and that she would remain the instructor. I told her that I was moving Sections 2 and 3 to Wednesdays and Fridays. Section 2 would run 2:00 - 3:15 and section 3 would run 3:30 - 4:45.

"You can't do that," she said.

"Scheduling is the prerogative of the department head," I reminded her.

"With the permission of the faculty," she replied.

"With *input* from the faculty. Which is what I'm trying to give you. Tell me what days and times you want to teach the sections, and so long as they are all different, I will accept your input."

"Forget about it. I'm not changing those sections and neither are you. There are no available classrooms at this point, so you can't change anything."

I ignored the classroom issue and told her I would assign sections 2 and 3 to other teachers if she refused to meet the classes as newly scheduled.

~

I drove back to Old Town and entered La Placita, taking a chair at the table by the big tree inside the building because it's one of the stations usually assigned to Susannah.

She brought me a menu and said,

"Shouldn't you be in your office, Mister Department Head?"

"I'm here on official business."

"Does the business involve choosing between red and green?"

"The official business is offering you a job teaching two sections of ART 2000 this semester as an adjunct. But since I'm here and it's lunchtime, I'll have the green chile."

"Are you serious?"

"Of course. You know I usually choose green."

She ignored my attempt at humor and said, "Are you serious about me *teaching*?" She looked like a ten-year-old girl who's just been promised a pony.

"Completely serious. The classes meet on Wednesdays and Fridays from 2:00 - 3:15 and 3:30 - 4:45."

She frowned. "I can't be there by 2:00. My shift ends at 2:30, and I can't jeopardize my job here."

"Can you teach the one that starts at 3:30?"

"Absolutely. This is so exciting. And I don't even mind not having both sections. It might even be better not to. I've never taught before, and I don't know if I could handle two sections in addition to waitressing."

"Okay. The 3:30 section is yours."

"Do you still want the green chile stew for

lunch?"

"Yes."

While I waited for my lunch, I looked over the list of possible adjuncts suggested by the students who needed the digital art class during the day. The only name I recognized was Raul Zamoria, a student who'd been in my fall class, ART 2330 Anasazi Pottery Methods. He did well as a potter and seemed to know everything about art history. But I had no idea if he knew anything about digital art. And on top of that, he was an undergraduate.

After lunch, I walked the two and a half blocks to Spirits in Clay, called Raul on my landline, got his voice mail, and left him a message.

Then I offered the 2:00 section of ART 2000 to Freddie. I was beginning to feel like a wheeler-dealer.

He stared at me. "You can't hire an ex-con."

"Like you said, I memorized the handbook. Hiring someone who is under indictment for a felony is not allowed. But ex-cons are not mentioned."

"Maybe because they thought that was obvious. And I didn't say you *memorized* the handbook; I said you *read* it. But I guess in your case it's the same thing."

I nodded. "Whit says I have an 'encyclopedia' mind."

"That's closer than he usually comes to the right word. Have you told anyone about offering me an adjunct position?"

"No."

"You need to do that."

"Who should I tell?"

"The dean."

I decided not to tell Dean Gangji and rely instead on the management adage that it's often better to ask for forgiveness rather than permission.

I used my old land line to call Tristan. As you already know, he is my first cousin once removed, but I think of him as my nephew, and he calls me Uncle Hubie. He's a perpetual student at UNM and earns a living doing computer stuff for people like me who can't or don't want to learn how to do it themselves. I fall into both categories – can't and don't want to. Despite being in his mid-twenties, he has a layer of baby fat. He also has dark eyes and black unkempt hair that hangs down in ringlets. Girls find him irresistible, although I suspect it's mainly because he's a nice person.

I asked him to meet me at my office and explained what I needed. Or started to explain. He figured it out before I finished my sentence and was sitting behind my desk when I got back to campus.

He looked up and said, "UNM uses Banner

educational software to manage everything from admissions to financial aid to grade reports, you name it. I've got the scheduling module up and running using your password."

"I don't have a password."

"You do now. It's *Techphobe1.*"

"Thanks."

"I figured you'd want something easy to remember."

I watched as he changed the days and times for sections 2 and 3 of Art 2000.

He asked what I wanted in the 'room' field. Bakke was right. There were no rooms available. I told him to enter ART 202.

"That's this office," he said.

"As of tomorrow, it's no longer an office; it's a classroom."

"Where will you work?"

"I'll go back to the office I had in the fall."

"The closet-sized one?"

I nodded. He shrugged and asked what I wanted in the 'instructor' field. I told him to enter 'Blass' for section 2 and 'Inchaustigui' for section 3.

"Playing matchmaker?" he asked.

Oops. I hadn't thought of that. I may have an encyclopedic mind, but I'm also frequently inattentive to the obvious.

I penciled the following message to Bakke: "This is to confirm that you declined to teach sections 2 and 3 of ART 2000 at the times I scheduled them for this semester despite the fact that they did not conflict with your schedule. As a result, your salary will be reduced for this semester by 50% since you are teaching half of the required course load. If you wish, I will schedule you for 2 courses in the mid-semester and one course in the summer session. The two mid-semester courses will make up for the two you are short this semester. In that case, your salary for this semester will not be reduced. And you will be paid for the summer course at the standard summer school rate."

Tristan sent the message as an email from my department head email, and he explained how to do it as he went through the steps. I now had it on record that I had made a reasonable offer to Bakke, but I didn't think I wanted to learn any more about emails.

"I need a secretary."

Tristan smiled and said, "Sorry, but I'm not available."

"Okay. But I have to have you here tomorrow."

I asked him to make the extreme sacrifice.

"You want me to be here at eight in the morning!"

"I'll have breakfast tacos and lots of coffee."

"Better bring them to my apartment. I can sleep right through the alarm clock."

Chapter 18

And he did. Which didn't matter because I have a key to his place. The coffee and dozen breakfast tacos were from Taqueria Mexico up on Lomas. I was there when they opened at 7:00 and on my way by 7:10 down to Tristan's apartment just south of the campus. The *cocineros* at Taqueria Mexico are as efficient as the ones at Frontier.

After I shook him awake, he inhaled 2 tacos and a cup of coffee on his way to the shower and three tacos and another coffee after he was dressed.

The students were gathered in the hall. Tristan has a stronger voice than I do and more confidence. He told them to have their ID number ready. He sat down at my desk. The first student stepped up and Tristan typed as the student said "8705467933. Section 3."

While Tristan was registering students, Raul Zamoria walked into the office. I told you he's brilliant. Also organized. Has great posture and exudes confidence. But – to be blunt – the guy is ugly, acne scars, a crooked chin, and a heavy brow being the main issues. But he was well-liked by the other students in my class which I hope proves that we have moved away from judging people by their appearance, a move not yet made by Hollywood.

We shook hands and he said, "Got your message that you wanted to talk with me. I heard you're the acting head of the department. Struck me as odd, but if the fall semester proved anything, it's that nothing is ever normal in the art department. What is it you want to talk about?"

"Some students were complaining about digital art being taught only in the evening. I told them if they could recommend someone to teach it, I'd try to hire that person as an adjunct. You are one of the people they recommended."

"Sure. I'll teach that course during the day."

I hesitated, and he said, "But first you want to know if I'm qualified."

"Right."

"I earned a B.S. in computer science from New Mexico State five years ago and took a job at Terameg, a tech firm here in Albuquerque. It was boring and I've always loved art, so I enrolled to get a second degree, a B.A. in art. The guy who teaches the course in the evening – Paul Ethan – also works at Terameg. He paid me to develop the syllabus for him. It's basically my course. I got my B.A. in art at the December graduation, and I'm now in the graduate program. So I can teach as a T.A."

"What's a T.A.?"

"It stands for teaching assistant, which is what they call a graduate student who teaches."

By the time Raul and I had reached an agreement, Tristan had enrolled fifty-one students in the two courses of ART 2000, 25 in section 2 and 26 in section 3. I gave him his next task, creating two daytime sections of the digital art class with Raul Zamoria as the instructor.

Then I had him pull up the staffing part of Banner and create adjunct contracts for Susannah, Freddie, and a T.A. contract for Raul.

If you're wondering about the propriety of hiring friends and skipping equal opportunity and affirmative action regulations, it's a common practice. Emergency temporary hires of adjuncts and T.A.s are exempt because they are often hired on the day of their first class. Running a search process is simply not feasible.

After all the new classes were created, students registered and adjuncts hired, I realized why Freddie had made fun of me for wondering how I would stay busy and earn my pay.

Tristan opened the bag of tacos, gave me three and took the remaining four. I brewed coffee in the fancy coffeemaker that was one of the perks of the department head's office.

While we ate, I told Tristan about Gurney Guy and he said, "So we have a relative neither of us knew about?"

"I never knew about him, but I was hoping you might."

"I suppose my father could have had a child with someone other than my mother, but that person wouldn't share DNA with you."

"Right," I said and nothing more. I didn't feel comfortable asking him if his mother rather than his father might have had a child he didn't know about. But of course he thought of that possibility himself.

"I suppose my mother could have had a child before she met my father. Or even after my father died. Obviously I don't remember anything about the first couple of years of my life. But I don't think Gurney Guy is my half-brother. My mother thinks secrecy is kin to witchcraft. She tells everybody everything. I can't imagine her not telling me if she had another child. And I also can't imagine her giving up a child. She kept me even though she was widowed while still in the hospital maternity ward recovering from giving birth."

"Do you know if anyone suggested that she give you up?"

"According to mom, almost everyone suggested it. Remember she eloped with my father the first night they met, so it's not like she was prepared to raise and support a child. And single mothers were not so well regarded back then as they are today."

"I'm glad she kept you."

"Me, too."

I was biting into a taco when Tristan again made me aware of my inattentiveness by asking how I planned to get 26 students and an instructor in my office.

Art 2000 is a lecture course. No need for easels or work tables. The office would hold the classes except for one problem – a desk so large that it should have 'HMS Dreadnaught' painted on its prow.

I remembered Freddie advising me to mollify Bakke. I went to Hockley's office and made a pact with him. Then I walked to Bakke's office and said, "I've decided I want to get rid of the big desk in my office. Hockley wants it, but I thought I should offer it to you first."

She squinted at me. "Why?"

"It's just too big for me. It feels awkward sitting behind the thing."

She gave me a condescending look. "I meant why offer it to me first?"

"He already has a bigger office than you do."

"A bigger studio, too," she noted.

With more students in it, I thought to myself.

She said she wanted the desk. I asked her if she wanted it in her studio or office, and she surprised me by choosing her office.

I recruited six husky students to carry the

thing. It took them an hour to get the desk into Bakke's office because they first had to remove her old desk and all the cabinets and chairs in order to have room to maneuver it into place. She wanted the desk against the window, but it was too long to fit. So they had to orient it parallel to the window.

Then the office door wouldn't close. The door opened into the office and had obviously been open when the desk was brought it. But with the huge desk in place, there was not enough room for the door to swing back to the closed position.

The students brought woodworking tools from the 3-D studio. Under the direction of Hal Olley, they removed the office door, removed the hinges, chiseled new mortices on the hall edge of the doorframe, and reinstalled the door so that it opened out into the hall instead of into the office.

Even though the office door no longer hit the desk, the file cabinet doors to each side of the door did. So the cabinets had to be lifted over the desk in order to be placed against the side walls of the office.

This saga was reported to me by Tristan who seemed to enjoy being a sidewalk superintendent.

I stopped by Bakke's office at the end of the day and found her wedged so tightly behind the desk that having her head and arms in stocks would not have made her less mobile.

But she was smiling. "Hockley came by to see the desk. Even tried to talk me out of it. Thanks for giving it to me."

"You're welcome," I said.

"Also," she said, "I got your email. I still think it was a mistake to break up my stacked courses, but I will accept your offer of the midsemester and summer school courses."

"Thanks. I'm sure you'll do a good job with those courses."

Chapter 19

Susannah stormed into *Dos Hermanas* and said, "You set me up!"

I just stared at her.

"Admit it," she said.

"Admit what?"

"That you set me up."

"I have no idea what you're talking about."

She sat down and signaled to Angie. "I shouldn't even have a margarita with you. I can't believe you did that."

"Here's an idea. Talk to me in Basque. I wouldn't understand any of it, but at least I'd know why."

"Are you going to deny that you set me up to meet Freddie?"

"Yes. I deny it."

"So it's just coincidence that his class is directly before mine and in the same room? You did that on purpose because you knew he and I would cross paths."

What I immediately thought was *Oops*. What I said was, "Actually, *you* are responsible for that. Remember I offered you both sections? If you'd taken them, Freddie wouldn't be teaching."

Angie brought our drinks, and we both took

big sips.

Susannah calmed down a bit but still wanted to put some of the blame on me. She said, "Couldn't you at least have put his section or mine somewhere else?"

"There were no rooms available. I had to put both sections in my office."

"I thought that room looked familiar. What happened to the desk?

"I gave it to Bakke."

She frowned. "Why?"

I explained that Bakke had all three sections of ART 2000 as "stacked classes" and that most students who needed the course couldn't register for it because there were no options regarding time. When I told Freddie I was going to change the times and take two of the sections away from her, he suggested I try to mollify Bakke.

"You thought giving her an oversized desk would placate her?"

"I did and it did."

"I know she's weird, but not so weird that a desk would make up for losing two courses."

"It's not the desk. It's the fact that I did something for her."

"I don't get it. She doesn't even like you."

"True. As part of my accounting major, I had to take a management course. One thing we studied was the Hawthorn Effect."

"What? Bakke had a scarlet A on her pinafore?"

"Funny. But the effect wasn't named after Nathaniel. It was called that because a sociologist named Mayo ran an experiment in a Western Electric factory in the Chicago suburb of Hawthorne."

"Let me guess," she said, smiling. "They didn't want to call it the 'Mayo Effect' because that was reserved for the lunch experiment."

"Right. The lighting in the work area for one group of workers was made brighter while another group's lighting remained unchanged. The productivity of the workers with the brighter lighting increased."

"Mayo had to run an experiment to prove that?"

"Sounds like common sense, right. But then later, the workers' productivity increased when the lights were made *dimmer,* back to what they had been to begin with. So Mayo's conclusion was that what improved morale and therefore productivity was not *what* was done but was instead the fact that *something* was done. The theory being that any change in the workplace shows that management cares about the workers."

"So if you'd given her a filing cabinet instead of a desk, that would have made her just as happy?"

"Exactly. Maybe even happier, although that's not part of the Hawthorne Effect."

"Why would the filing cabinet have been better?"

"The desk is so big that she has to sort of crawl over one edge of it to get into her office."

"Your making this all up to get me off the subject of you setting me up to run into Freddie."

"No. I'd love to talk about it. How was the reunion?"

"I don't want to talk about it."

"Okay. How was your first class as a teacher?"

"Terrible. I had worked out in my mind exactly what I was going to say to them. But running into Freddie upset me so much that I forget everything I'd planned to say. I stammered and stuttered and finally just passed out the syllabuses I'd prepared and told them to read them before the next class."

"The plural is *syllabi,*" I noted.

"So do both of us a favor and fire me," she said and teared up.

I felt terrible. "No. I should fire the department head. When Tristan was entering the schedule changes for me, I told him to list Blass for Section 2 and Inchaustigui for Section 3, and he said, 'Matchmaking?' That should have been enough for me to think to alert you, but it wasn't because I just sometimes miss the obvious. I'm sorry, Suze."

She dabbed her eyes with a napkin she'd used to wipe a bit of salsa from her lips. "Damn. I got some chile juice in my eyes. Well, at least I have an excuse for crying. When I saw Freddie in the hall of the art building, I burst out in tears for no reason."

I shook my head. "There was a reason. You just haven't yet figured out what it was."

"Probably. He looked like a different person. Not physically – I already knew from the glimpse I got of him here on Saturday evening that his hair had gone white and he was thinner. But there was another sort of change … I don't know what to call it."

"His countenance," I suggested.

She nodded.

I said, "When Charles told me the facial recognition software popped up pictures of me as similar to Gurney Guy, I wondered why I didn't notice that he looked like me. The answer is that looking like someone is not just about having the same hair color or nose shape. It's about countenance – how your personality shows on your face. Dead people don't have countenance. What you noticed about Freddie is that he's changed inside."

"That's what you've been trying to tell me. But I didn't want to hear it." She was silent for a minute then asked, "How do you read his new countenance?"

"I'm not good at this, remember? I'm the guy who didn't think to warn you. I can memorize a page of a dictionary in a minute, but I don't always pick up on social stuff."

"You're better at it than you think. Look at how you knew some of the guys I dated were wrong for me, and I only discovered it later. Ice, for example. And Chris."

"Neither of those took much social insight. In Ice's case, the name gave it away, and Chris made a pass at me rather than you," I said and she laughed. Then she became serious and asked me again about the new Freddie.

"The old Freddie was glib. Now he's thoughtful, slower to comment. He's no longer the life of the party. He's long term instead. He's promoting others instead of himself."

"How do changes like that happen?"

"My guess is it has to do with responsibility. He always used painting as a way to promote himself and his career. But when he started teaching the inmates and saw how it was changing them, that became more important than his own work. I guess a cynical view might be that he couldn't promote himself while he was in jail, so being in prison was part of it. But the way he talked about teaching them, and the way the corrections officials praised his work and how much it changed some of the other prisoners, I have to think that's the foundation of the new Freddie."

"You ever experience that in anyone else?"

"No. But there's a similar case in the book I'm reading. Edith Warner and Tilano became godparents to a young couple who were married in the little house at Otowi, and Church describes it this way:

~

> To Tilano this meant far more than a perfunctory legal act. It meant that he had in the most true and serious sense become godfather to young Peter and Earle Miller; that Edith was now their godmother. Their duty toward them both was that of spiritual guidance. Among most Indian people there is a custom that a child is initiated into manhood by a ceremonial father or mother. He is "reborn" out of the closely protected circle of his parental family into the responsible life of the tribe to which he belongs. He is made aware, by a vividly enacted symbolic drama, of the reciprocal powers of life and death, and of his own function as man in the rhythmic pattern of existence.

~

"Peter and Earle? A gay couple got married

way back then?"

"The woman was named Peter. Don't ask me why."

"This is tough, Hubie. If Freddie is a changed man and a good one, I should be interested in him. But if he's really a different man, then he's not the guy I used to date and thought I loved. He's just a stranger. And older than me – remember that conversation about age we had when we first met?"

I nodded.

"And while I wouldn't say he's ugly, an old stranger with white hair and a crooked nose is not exactly a heartthrob. God, I sound so shallow."

"It's not shallow to care about someone's looks unless that's *all* you care about. I flirted with you that first time in this bar because you're a knockout. But if we had dated and I discovered you were shallow or mean or something, I wouldn't have hung on to you just to have a trophy girlfriend."

"'Trophy girlfriend' – I like the sound of that. But you have one now."

"Yes I do."

"What about Freddie?"

"There are many things you two have in common."

"Such as?"

"Art and murder mysteries."

"I don't remember him reading murder mysteries."

"Even better than reading them, he was in one!"

"Groan. I can't believe you said that. How am I supposed to introduce him, 'Here's my boyfriend who went to prison for murder'?"

"Manslaughter."

"Splitting hairs."

"I'll bet murder mysteries don't think of it as splitting hairs."

"How would you know? You don't read them."

"Right. And sometimes I think I'm the only person in New Mexico who doesn't. When I mentioned to Charles your suggestion that Gurney Guy might have been stabbed with an icicle, he asked me if I'd been reading Simon Brett."

"That's great. Even an FBI agent reads them."

"All that proves is he *knows* about them."

"How would he know about them if he didn't read them?"

"Easy. Check out this list." I closed my eyes and pictured a bookshelf at Bookworks, one of Albuquerque's independent bookstores located conveniently next door to a Flying Star cafe. "Sandi Ault, Joseph Badal, Amy Bennett, Steve Brewer, Marie Romero Cash, Alice Duncan, J.L.

Greger, Steven Havill, Darynda Jones, Robert Kidera, Robert Kresge, Michael McGarrity, Pari Noskin Taichert, Judith Van Gieson, and Patrica Smith Wood."

I opened my eyes and said, "All mystery writers right here in New Mexico. Sometimes I think I'm not only the only person in the state who doesn't read them – I'm also the only person who doesn't *write* them."

"Then how do you know all the names of … oh, your 'encyclopedia' mind. And you see them at bookstores when you're looking for the weird stuff you read like New Mexico history."

"Exactly."

"But you have read some murder mystery authors."

"Nope."

"Yep. You've read Rudolfo Anaya."

"Of course. He almost singlehandedly launched contemporary Hispanic fiction with the publication of *Bless Me, Ultima*. But he doesn't write murder mysteries."

"Yes he does. He wrote a series of murder mysteries featuring Sonny Baca, a private investigator. And you've also read Tony Hillerman."

I laughed. "The only things I ever read by Hillerman were his syllabus and some exam questions he wrote. I took a journalism course from him when I was an undergraduate, but that was before he started writing mysteries. And before you ask, I've also read some things by his daughter, Anne. She's a journalist. Most people have read something she wrote, but the only book I read by her was the one she did with her husband, Don Strel, *Tony Hillerman's Landscapes: Southwest Guide & Map*."

"You used the maps to hunt down pots?"

"I'll plead the 5th on that."

Susannah said, "Here are some New Mexico murder mystery writers you missed: Amanda Allen, Pamela Christie, Sarah Lovett, Mary Oerter-Kirschner, Jonathan Miller, Ann Myers, Aileen Schumacher, Connie Shelton, Susan Slater, Aimée & David Thurlo, and Robert Westbrook."

"And I thought I had a good memory. I guess there aren't enough real jobs in New Mexico, so people have to resort to writing books."

"This from a guy who reads several books a week?"

Chapter 20

"Look," Sharice said, "antelope!"

We were in Torrance County driving along County Road A099 which I'd reached by taking the old Route 66 east through Tijeras Canyon and then connecting with A099 near Moriarity.

I'll do almost anything to avoid Interstate 40.

"This would be a great place for self-driving cars," Sharice said. "You could be looking at the antelopes instead of staring at the road."

"I know men are not supposed to be good at multi-tasking, but I can drive and see antelope at the same time."

She laughed and said, "But think how relaxing it would be just to stare at the scenery and not have to drive."

"Sitting in a car being driven by a computer would not be relaxing; it would be terrifying. I'd be poised to grab the steering wheel in case the car started veering off the road."

She shook her head. "Self-driving cars are less likely to run off the road than ones being driven by humans. They're fitted with lots of cameras that see the edge of the road, the lane markers, curves, and things like that. Since the computer never gets distracted or tired, it's more reliable than humans."

"Until some prankster repaints a stretch of lane markers so that they that veer into oncoming traffic."

"The computers are probably programmed to recognize when a lane marker is abnormal. Software can be pretty smart, Hubie."

"Right. Like the facial recognition software that compared me to Floss Man."

"Makes my point. You and he *are* related, and the software picked up on that before you did. And I know you like looking at the wide-open New Mexico vistas."

"Self-driving cars are the worst invention since the clap-on clap-off lamp. People who want to stare out at the scenery instead of driving don't need self-driving cars. They need a bus ticket. But I have to admit this road would be a good place to test self-driving cars because when they run off the road, there's nothing to hit."

"True. Yet the bareness is part of the appeal."

"Edith Warner had that same view. She said, 'No wooded, verdant country could make me feel as this one does. Its very nudity makes it intimate. There are only shadows to cover its bareness. I think I could not bear again great masses of growing things. It would stifle me as buildings do'."

"You quoting from memory?"

"Paraphrasing. But I think it's close."

"Does the condo stifle you?"

"No. The expansive view of the mountains is great, and the place is so open and minimalist. Except for your closet."

"I've added only one new dress since you moved in."

"How did you stuff it in there?"

"It's not *that* crowded."

"I suppose you're right. There's still enough space to slip in a slip if you push hard."

"Nobody wears slips anymore. Why are we getting back on the freeway?"

"Because this is the last interchange. This road ends in the middle of nowhere."

"I thought we'd already passed the middle of nowhere."

"I stand corrected. This road ends at the *end* of nowhere. We have to take I-40 from here to Tucumcari."

"Tucumcari is a funny word, like *nincompoop* or *smithereens*. Does it mean something?"

"Tristan told me it's from a Comanche word, *Tukamukaru*, which means to lie in wait to ambush someone."

"Why would a town choose a name like that?"

"Maybe they saw it as a step up from the

original name, *Six-Shooter Siding*."

"You're kidding, right?"

"Nope. It started as a rowdy railroad town full of saloons and dance-hall girls."

"What's it like now?"

"Well, let's just say that Edith Warner would probably like it. It's barren and most of the buildings that might stifle her are empty."

"It's almost a ghost town?"

"No. There's maybe five thousand people there. But you might say it's a ghost of its previous self. It boomed when Route 66 was constructed. Route 66 was Main Street; it passed right through the middle of town. Motels, cafes and curio shops prospered. But when Interstate 40 was built, it bypassed the town. Millions of people drive by Tucumcari every year. But the only ones who stop are the Mother Roaders."

"Mother Roaders?"

"A small but devout group of travelers – most on motorcycles – who are fascinated with Route 66, also known as the Main Street of America and the Mother Road."

"Is it that fascinating?"

"Let's see what you think."

"So my job is to see if Junior and or her mother looks like you and whether Route 66 is fascinating."

"And to approve the motel I've selected," I replied.

We eventually pulled in next to the Safari Motel sign topped by a 3-D plastic camel with a rider wearing a Yasser-Arafat-style head covering. Yasser would not have approved of this politically incorrect image of an Arab, but it's hard to be offended by something so obviously kitschy.

Another plastic camel graced the registration area. Sharice stared at it as I registered.

The Safari is about a mile from Junior's small frame house on West Railroad Avenue. Having been in the car for three hours, we decided to walk.

The most interesting thing on West Railroad Avenue was the old passenger station which is now a museum. The second most interesting thing was an automobile transmission repair shop with a damaged sign that read *Transmiss*. Given Tucumcari's conservative population, it's a safe bet the sign is not about gender.

The two most interesting things in the house, not counting Junior, were a tame racoon and pictures of Dana Andrews.

Junior greeted us at the door. I introduced her to Sharice. Junior hugged her and said, "Tristan has told me all about you. You are even prettier than he described."

Sharice blushed. "Your son is one of my favorite people. You must be very proud of him."

"I am," Junior replied. Then she looked at her watch and said, "Oh my goodness; it's almost 5:17." She thrust out her arms and covered Sharice's ears with her hands. I felt the room begin to shake. A roaring sound got louder as the shaking increased. Then I heard a train whistle change pitch as the locomotive sped by behind the house.

Junior released her grip on Sharice's head and said, "Sorry I didn't have time to warn you. How about some dandelion tea?"

"That would be lovely."

As Junior led us to the kitchen, Sharice smiled at me, and I relaxed.

As she poured the tea, Junior explained that the dandelions grow wild in her yard, so all she has to do is pick them and dry them. Then she added that the tea prevents water retention, lowers blood pressure, fights inflammation, controls blood sugar, and reduces cholesterol.

"I love dandelion greens in salads," Sharice said.

"You should never eat dandelions raw," Junior scolded. "They scratch the lining of your stomach."

"I didn't know that," Sharice said. "Thanks for telling me."

A photo of my Aunt Beatrice was taped to the refrigerator door. I pointed to it and asked when it was taken.

"It was taken by Rhino a few days before Tristan was born. We were on a picnic with Mom out at the lake."

I saw Sharice study the photo, which was why I'd asked about it.

"Something smells good," I said.

"Mushroom stir fry. I gathered the mushrooms yesterday in the foothills of the mountains."

My appetite disappeared. Junior is a good-hearted person, but not someone I would trust to distinguish an edible fungus from a poison one. After a moment's reflection, I realized I am also someone I would not trust to distinguish an edible fungus from a poison one. That thought made me feel less guilty about not trusting Junior, but no less afraid of eating her mushrooms.

I was trying to think of an excuse for not eating the mushrooms when Junior set the bowl on the table. I looked at the dish and was happy I'd failed to think up an excuse not to eat it. I was staring down at morels, a species distinctive in appearance and obviously not poison. They are also one of my favorite foods even though I've had them less than a dozen times in my life. They're rarely available in stores, and when they are, they cost something like fifty dollars a pound.

"You could have made a lot of money selling these," I said.

"Money's not important, Hubie. And anyway, I don't know anyone else who eats them except for Tristan. Will you take the ones I didn't cook back for him?"

"Be glad to."

The racoon's left front paw was missing. He took turns begging for food between me and Sharice. She offered him a morel, and he tried to grasp it between his good paw and his stump, but it dropped to the floor. He was sniffing at it when Junior said, "Lucky, you know you don't like mushrooms. Now stop your begging,"

"Why did you name him Lucky?" Sharice asked.

"Because when the train ran over his paw, he came to my back door. If he'd gone to anyone else on the street, they would have taken him to the animal shelter where he would have been put down. But I took him in and bandaged him up."

"Does he ever go outside?"

"He used to want out when any of the local females were in heat. But after I had him fixed, he's been content to stay around."

I swallowed the impulse to laugh when Sharice gave me a get-hold-of-yourself look. Then I started thinking about how to introduce the topic of Floss Man.

Junior placed a bowl of figs on the table and said, "So you want to know if Tristan is my only child."

It wouldn't surprise me if she were psychic, but my guess was Tristan had warned her. Fair enough.

"I wouldn't phrase it that way," I said. "A man who was found dead in Old Town shares DNA with me, and I have no idea who he is. What I want to know is whether you know anyone related to us that I don't know about. The FBI suggested the dead man could have been another child that my mother or father had. Or for all I know, my father had a brother he never mentioned, a black sheep so to speak. So the question is not as specific as whether you had a child in addition to Tristan; it's whether you know something about our family tree that I don't."

She pondered if for a minute or two. "I don't know of any black sheep or lost relatives. But there is one thing. Did you know that when you were born, your father was on a sabbatical?"

"He was quite the researcher," I replied. "He was granted many sabbaticals and published in various scholarly journals. But I didn't know that one of his sabbaticals was when I was born."

"So he was away from your mother for an entire semester. Maybe he had a brief affair that resulted in a child."

"I don't think my father would have done that."

"People do things we don't expect. We all have moments of weakness."

"He wouldn't have abandoned a child, even one born out of wedlock."

"Maybe he never knew the woman was pregnant."

"Wouldn't she have told him?"

She shrugged. "She might not have known for a month or longer. Maybe he was gone by then, and she had no way of contacting him. Didn't know his last name."

"A one-night stand? No last names? I can't believe—"

"It happens, Hubie. Believe me. I know. I never had a second child. But I could have because I've sometimes had unprotected sex. I'm wiser now."

I now appreciated Tristan's claim that his mother was incapable of keeping secrets.

Before we left, I brokered an exchange of gifts between mother and child. I gave her cash in an envelope and told her it was from Tristan. Which was partially true; he provided the envelope.

She asked me to take a gift to Tristan, a locket she had made from pull tabs people had thrown in her yard.

~

"So your father's hypothetical scorned brother was a 'black sheep'. If I had a brother like that, would he be a 'white sheep'?"

We were walking back to the Safari Motel. A strong north wind was blowing and Sharice was clinging to me for warmth.

"Sorry. That was an insensitive thing for me to say."

She smiled at me. "Can't you tell when I'm kidding? I guess the PC crowd might think it's racial, but I just see it as nature. The black sheep is rare. And therefore special. And why did you almost laugh after Junior mentioned having the racoon fixed?"

"Because there's an old story – almost certainly made up – that an entry in the pets section of the classified ads read: "Lost dog. Blind in one eye, missing front right leg, recently castrated. Answers to the name Lucky."

"And Lucky the racoon almost fits the description of the lost dog."

"Right."

She shrugged.

I asked her if Junior or the picture of her mother Bea looks like me.

"All white people look the same," she said and laughed. "Junior looks more like you than she does Tristan. Maybe they nicknamed his father Rhino because his genes were so strong."

"But does she look like me?"

"Well, if I'd just seen her walking down the street and didn't know who she is, I wouldn't have thought, *Gee, she looks like Hubie*. But it wouldn't be a total surprise to find out that you two are related. And the photo of your aunt Bea looks like the picture you showed me of your mother, but again not so much that I'd have pegged her as your relative ."

"Aunt Bea and my mother did look like sisters. They were both tall and thin, same facial shape, same hair and eyes, but at the same time, there was a difference. Not anything physical like one of them having a big nose. I guess it was that countenance thing again. Aunt Bea was like Junior, guileless and unconcerned with social norms. She had a relaxed this-is-who-I-am look. My mother was more on the prim and proper side."

"What do you think of Junior's idea that your father's sabbatical might explain Floss Man?"

"Not buying it. My father had a sabbatical when I was in high school and another when I was living in the dorm. In both cases, my mother went with him."

"Maybe she didn't go on the sabbatical when she was pregnant because she had to stay in Albuquerque to have check-ups with her obstetrician."

Having no idea about the protocols for pregnant women half a century ago, I made no comment. Instead, I asked Sharice what she thought of Junior.

"I like her. She's her own woman. But what's the deal with Dana Andrews?"

"Junior went into a deep depression after Tristan was born, a combination she now says of post-partum and grief about Rhino. My Aunt Beatrice raised Tristan for the first year or so of his life. Junior immersed herself in films, watching them twenty hours a day between four hours of fitful sleep. Then she saw a film called *Strange Lady in Town* about a woman doctor from Boston who comes to New Mexico in the 1880s to introduce modern medicine. The local doc, played by Andrews, doesn't think women can be doctors and makes fun of her newfangled device, the stethoscope. But she eventually wins him over, and he even teaches her to ride a horse, telling her as she struggles to 'sit up straight and try not to look like a sack of potatoes'. She thought Dana Andrews was delivering that line to her, so she started sitting up straight and not being a sack of potatoes. She took long walks, holding her head high and her chin out. And she began to recover."

"Probably the exercise and the fresh air." Sharice snuggled even closer to me as we walked quickly to our warm room. "Does that story remind you of someone you know and love."

"You when you were saving money for a mastectomy."

"That wasn't all I was saving."

The other thing she was saving was a drug called midazolam. She had access to it because it is sometimes used to sedate dental patients. In larger doses it has been used to execute murderers.

I pulled her closer and said, "That was one of the items on your list of things you had to tell me before our romance could become serious. And as I recall, it was also on the list of things we were never again to speak of."

"Strange thing about that list. Now that we're a couple, there's nothing we can't talk about – even castrated animals."

"Sharing everything is part of being a family. So I can tell you that Floss Man is morphing into Bogeyman. I'd like to talk about it, but I don't know what to say. There's nothing specific. Just constant dread. I don't know of what. Maybe of not knowing."

"Suppose you wrote a book called *The Floss Man Murder*."

"If I did, I'd fit right in with the dozens of other New Mexicans writing murder mysteries."

"What would be the key to the story?"

"The lab person accidentally labeled

someone else's DNA as mine and the whole thing was a big mistake."

"Good ending. Now write one that might actually be the case."

"I like the black sheep version. My father and his brother were both suitors for my mother's affection. When she chose my father, Uncle Cain ran away and was never heard from again. He got married and had a son about my age. He never told the son about his uncle who was my father. But after Cain died, his son – Floss Man – found out somehow and decide to get in touch with me, the cousin he never knew. He wanted to wear an orchid in his lapel for his visit, and fell on a garden stake while cutting the orchid. He didn't think the wound was serious. He had happy thoughts about meeting me until the wound opened and he bled to death, which is relatively painless."

"Bravo! Great story. I like that you named your uncle *Cain*. Got another version?"

"There's still the 'my Aunt Beatrice was switched with another baby in the hospital nursery theory'. That means my mother's real sister ended up with another couple. When she grew up, she got married and had children. Floss Man is either her son or her grandson."

"Another good story. But after all these years, there's surely no way to verify it."

"Actually, there is." I fished the locket out of

my pocket. "What do you suppose is in this?"

"Junior's picture?"

"Maybe. What else might it be?"

She smiled. "A lock of her hair?"

We had reached the motel. After we got inside and took off our jackets, we opened the locket. It was indeed a bit of hair. The desk in the room had envelopes with the Safari camel sign on the upper left where the sender's address would be. I took a bit of the hair and sealed it in one of the envelopes, leaving the rest in the locket.

Sharice guessed that I was going to have Charles Webbe compare the DNA in Junior's hair with my DNA. "What about HIPAA?" she asked.

"Who is Hippa? Rhino's brother?"

She ignored my pun and said, "HIPAA stands for Health Insurance Portability and Accountability Act. It forbids the sharing of people's health information without their permission."

"I'm not going to tell anyone about her DNA. All I want to know is if she's actually related to me."

"If she's not, will you tell her?"

Good question. "You're a health care professional. You understand HIPAA. You tell me."

"Forget HIPAA. It applies only to healthcare

professionals and institutions like hospitals and health insurance companies. This is about you and Junior."

"If we are related, which I suppose is likely the case, I don't think I'll tell her. What would be the point? But if we aren't related ..."

"Sticky, right? On the one hand you might think she deserves to know the truth. But on the other, think how weird it would be for her to discover that your mother was not really her aunt."

"Maybe it wouldn't be all that traumatic for her. She and my mother were not particularly close. And her mother is still her biological mother and her son is still her biological son. On the other hand, maybe it would be better not to tell her. Why upset long-held beliefs? The point is to find out how Floss Man is related to me, not to interfere in Junior's world."

Chapter 21

I guess it's time to explain Freddie's quip that he didn't want to return to Rio Grande Lofts because of security issues revealed by my breaking in. I don't think he mentioned I did so seven times.

I had a good reason, perhaps even a noble one. I intended to retrieve and return sacred pots stolen from the Ma people of San Roque Pueblo. On my first visit, I got through the secure gate at the basement garage in the evening, slept in my Bronco, and then got past another security gate at the elevator in the morning. I expected a solo ride to the top floor because I was reverse commuting. All the residents would be headed down.

But the elevator stopped at the fourth floor, and the doors slid open to reveal a stunning young woman with impressively coiffed blond hair.

"Going down?" she asked

"Up," I replied and reached for the 'close door' button.

"I'll ride along," she said and stepped in before I could get the door closed. "Why are you going up at this time of morning?"

I gave her a wan smile and patted my

pockets. "Forgot my keys."

"Looks like you forgot your iron, too," she said flatly. Spending the night in the Bronco had taken a toll on my appearance.

She struck me as a take-charge person who would not hesitate to call security if she spotted someone suspicious in the building, and I figured I fell into that category. "Sorry," I said, "ever since my wife left me, I've been sort of disheveled. I have no idea how to iron. In fact, I think she took the iron."

It was a lame story, but I'm not good at improv.

"Why did she leave you?" she asked, unabashed.

"She met a younger man."

She seemed to relax slightly.

The elevator reached the eleventh floor and I stepped out. She stuck her foot against the door.

"Did she take your razor, too?" The woman had no shame. Then she smiled. "What's your name?"

"Hubert."

She laughed. "I'm Stella, but of course you already know that. If you need to borrow an iron, just ask. I might even show you how to use it."

I missed two covert elements in that conversation. In case you are no better at hidden messages than I am, I'll tell you what they were. The first surface message was my fumbling attempt to misrepresent myself. The hidden message was that the person I pretended to be was irresistible to Stella and, Susannah later explained, to many other women as well. I had inadvertently fed Stella a great pick-up line.

The second surface message was that Stella felt sorry for me and was willing to lend me her iron and instruct me on its use. The hidden message – again explained to me by Susannah – was that Stella was flirting with me.

Since I broke in six more times, you already realize I didn't find the purloined pots that first morning. My second trip to Rio Grande Lofts did not involve surreptitious entry. Stella let me in as a guest. She used one of her blouses to demonstrate how to iron. It was the blouse she had been wearing moments before the lesson began. One thing led to another as they tend to do when a woman disrobes in front of a guy who hasn't had sex in several years.

Stella turned out to be Channel 17's Roving Reporter, which is why she assumed I knew who she was. I didn't because I don't have a television.

You may also recall – amazing how things can get so complicated – that I was briefly a suspect in the murder that happened in Rio Grande Lofts. The primary reason I was a suspect was Stella's report on the evening news. Standing in front of crime scene tape at Rio Grande Lofts, she reported that, "Hubert Schuze had been at the party, left the party, and then the partygoers hear a gunshot. When Schuze returned, he was covered with blood."

After hearing that, I was pretty certain I was back to doing my own ironing. But Stella and I eventually became friends.

Which is good because I was depending on her to help me out if hiring Freddie became an issue.

I called her on the Monday after Sharice and I returned from Tucumcari. She met me in my office.

"You said you're now the head of the art department. So why are you in a closet?"

"Enrollment increases in art classes made us run out of classrooms. So I gave up my office and made it a classroom."

"You want me to do a story on your magnanimous gesture?"

Stella's beautiful blue eyes would be beguiling were it not for the fact that she never blinks. Her reportorial style is head-on blunt. Like Geraldo Rivera but smarter and better looking.

"The story I thought you'd be interested in is that Freddie Blass is teaching art classes this semester."

"I thought he was in prison."

"He was released on the Saturday before classes began."

"How did he get hired so fast?"

"Like I said, enrollment is skyrocketing. We needed adjuncts and we needed them fast."

"Even ex-cons?"

"Especially ex-cons. Universities are about changing lives. For students and for teachers. Freddie paid his debt to society. He was a model prisoner and received a commendation from the Warden for the work he did in rehabilitating other inmates. We're giving him a second chance."

I was laying it on thick and she was staring into the hall.

"Why are those kids hanging around?"

"I told them Stella Ramsey would be here. They probably want a selfie with you."

She smiled. "Bullshit. You want then to encourage me to do a piece on Freddie."

I nodded. "Just talk to them."

~

I'd called Charles Webbe after I called Stella, and he showed up while she was chatting with the students. He asked me why I was still in the adjunct office.

"Trying to reduce my carbon footprint."

"Right. What you got for me?"

I handed him the envelope from the Safari

Motel. He peeked inside and said, "So you went to Tucumcari and got a hair sample from Tristan's mother, and you want to find out if she's actually related to you."

"The Tucumcari part was easy," I said. "But how'd you know the hair part and why I wanted it?"

"Because I've run through all the possibilities. One would be that the woman who you think was your Aunt Beatrice was not actually your aunt. And your real aunt is the mother or grandmother of the John Doe in the morgue. Babies being accidentally switched shortly after birth does happen. My favorite example is the Mark Twain story *The Tragedy of Pudd'nhead Wilson* in which two babies, one white and one black, are switched at birth, resulting in both passing for races that they are not. You and I are about the same age; maybe we were switched at birth."

"May be something to that. Just think, if I'd been switched and got your parents, maybe I'd have grown up big and strong."

"Yeah, but you'd still be white."

I asked him if switched babies is just an urban myth, and he surprised me by saying, "Approximately 25,000 babies are switched every year. Most of the mistakes are discovered before the parents leave the hospital, but many of them are not. 25,000 sounds like a lot, but there are 4 million births a year, so it's less than one in a thousand. But it does happen."

~

My next visitor was William Hughes, Assistant Director of the Office of Compliance, who said, "I am here to inform you that a complaint has been filed with my office by a faculty member who alleges that you violated the Equal Employment Opportunities Act."

He handed me a sealed envelope. "This is a copy of the complaint."

He handed me another envelope. "This is a copy of the procedure you are to follow in responding to the charge. Please note that neither the director nor the staff of the Office of Compliance with the Equal Employment Opportunities Act forms an opinion about any allegation until all parties have completed the required procedural steps."

I had heard this same spiel from Mr. Hughes during the fall semester except in that case it had been an allegation that I'd violated the Equal Education Opportunities Act and the complainant – is that a word? – had been a student. It's hard to walk the halls of academe these days without tripping over the initials of some act.

Mr. Hughes thrust a clipboard at me with a single paper under the clip. "Please sign here to acknowledge receipt of a copy of the complaint and the procedural process."

"No."

"No?"

"No."

"You aren't going to sign the form acknowledging receipt of a copy of the complaint and the procedural process?"

"I am not."

He stared at me for a few seconds. "I know you."

"Yes, you do."

"You also refused to sign a complaint last semester."

"Right."

"You know the process will go forward with or without your participation."

"I do know that. And I choose without."

He shook his head slowly. "What's wrong with you?"

"Nothing is wrong with me. You and I just look at things differently. I'm suspicious of large institutions, corporations, and government. I don't think legislation and cumbersome one-size-fits-all procedures are an effective way to assure justice and equality. My father was fond of saying that in the year I was born, the two most important things the government was involved in were Watergate and Viet Nam. I guess his distrust of institutions rubbed off on me. If Professor Armstrong has a problem, I would welcome him to come to me and talk about it person to person. I'd try my best to solve any problem he has."

"How do you know it's Armstrong?"

"Because he and I are both part of a small department. We know each other."

"Perhaps he feels he wouldn't be treated fairly by you."

"I suspect that's exactly how he feels. But he has no reason to believe that because he hasn't tried."

"You don't get to choose how he deals with his complaint. He makes that choice, and he chose to file an official complaint with us."

"Which is his right. And I have chosen not to participate, which is my right."

He stared at me for a few seconds then walked away.

~

Whit Fletcher passed Hughes in the hall, the only two men in the building in suits. "Someone is teaching a class in your office," Whit said.

"Former office."

"You been demoted back to adjunct already?"

"No. I just think classes are more important than offices."

"How about I buy you a cup of coffee?"

I found a table at Frontier and Whit bought

two coffees.

"You know about Crimestoppers?" he asked.

I nodded.

He said, "Big cities like Chicago and Miami pay five thousand or more for a tip that helps solve a murder. The Albuquerque branch pays a measly one thousand. Guess they factor in local cost of living."

"Or in this case, cost of dying. But the low payment doesn't affect you, Whit, because law enforcement personnel are not eligible."

"Which is where you come in. If I get a lead, I feed it to you and—"

"I know. I call it in and we split the reward. We worked that before, remember? Except you got the lion's share."

"Well, I did all the work."

"I don't know about doing it again. That time we got a dangerous person off the streets, and I used the money to help someone in need."

"I also used my part for someone in need. Birdie needed a 25th anniversary diamond. I coulda been an endangered species if I didn't produce that stone. You shoulda seen her examining it to make sure it wasn't one of those ziconimums. She was squinting so hard you coulda blindfolded her with dental floss."

"But this is a weird situation," I said. "The murdered guy – if he was murdered – is kin to me. Me providing a tip may be ... not a conflict of interest, not nepotism ... I don't know what to call it."

He shrugged. "What you should call it is a long shot. I been researching puncture wounds. Sent the guy's picture to every PD and Sherriff's office in the state. Sent uniformed guys to fancy men's shops in Albuquerque, Santa Fe, Denver and El Paso. Zilch. What I figure is the only way we solve this is if you figure it out. And we have some new info. The lab boys say the cause of death was blood loss caused by the laceration of the right external iliac artery. But they also found some poison in the wound." He pulled a paper from his shirt pocket and read the name to me. "Palytoxin."

"Never heard of it."

"Me neither. But the boys say it would have killed him if he hadn't bled to death."

"So I guess we can rule out accidental death."

"Yep. I figure the stabber was trying to poison the guy and just hit the artery by accident."

Chapter 22

I spent all day Tuesday working on my 12th day report and was a bit late getting home. Sharice and I generally have a coupe of Gruet and talk about how our days went. I didn't think the 12th day report would be of much interest, so I asked her to go first.

"No. You have to go first," she replied, "because after you hear my news, you'll be speechless."

"I worked on the 12th day report."

"Which is?"

"A summary of enrollments, changes to the published schedules, and expenditures related to the start of the semester."

"Why is it called the 12th day report?"

"Because the 12th day of class is when we peg the official enrollment number for every class."

"Why the 12th day?"

"Part of the funding from the legislature is based on enrollments. Since students add and drop classes, the numbers vary every day. So someone decided the 12th day would be the official day because it's long enough into the semester that we have time to take a count."

"So God created the universe in six days,

but it takes humans twice that long to count students?"

"Actually, the computer counts them. The Dean will have all the numbers at the meeting tomorrow. What he wants from the department heads is the reasons for the numbers – why they went up or down, why some sections were added and some cancelled, things like that. Boring, right? So what's your exciting news?"

She scooted over, put her arms around me, gave me a long and passionate kiss, then said, "I'm pregnant!"

"We're going to have a baby!"

She laughed. "That's what generally happens when a woman is pregnant."

"But it's less than a month since your last—"

"You are so behind the times. It's part of what I love about you. You and my Dad are alike in that way. He and you are going to become great buddies."

"But it's only the 21st."

"And we had sex without birth control on the 8th."

"So I got you pregnant the very first time we weren't using birth control?"

"Do I detect a little male ego in your voice?"

"No. Well… maybe. But I didn't think it would happen that night."

"Maybe it didn't. Maybe it was two nights later. But it did happen, and I hope you're as excited as I am."

"I am. And also sort of overwhelmed. We've created a new human being. That's a lot of responsibility."

"Which you're ready for, right?"

"Absolutely."

"And you remember that little rhyme," she asked. 'First comes love, then comes marriage, then come baby in the baby carriage'?"

"I do. And we can still get it in the right order if we get married before the baby is born."

"You're sure you want to marry me?"

"I've asked you fifteen times in the last year-and-a-half."

"Ask me again."

I jumped off the love seat, knelt in front of her, took her hand, and said the two simple words – 'Marry me'."

"Yes!"

"I'm going to love being your husband. And I'm going to love being a father. But I'm totally unprepared for that role. I've never even held a baby, much less tried to take care of one."

"You were also totally unprepared for being department head, but you figured that out. You're a quick study."

"Most of it is still a mystery to me. And the few things I figured out may or may not be right."

"According to the Channel 17 news, you're

already a legend among department heads."

I stared at her.

"I was watching the 5:00 o'clock news while waiting for you. Your former girlfriend, Stella, did a report on Freddie that made him out to be the best teacher in history and you to be a hero for hiring him. She even had a segment with a guy named Delatorre who talked about how Freddie helped rehabilitate fellow inmates via art lessons. I figure you put her up to it, right?"

"Guilty as charged. But I told her it was not about me, just about Freddie. And she was not my girlfriend."

She gave me a devilish smile. "Right. She was just a beautiful woman who seduced little innocent you by ironing in the nude."

"Exactly."

She laughed and said, "You were so cute when you told me about that."

"You made me do it."

"Yes I did. And I loved the way you squirmed. Like you're doing now. I'm not jealous of her, Hubie. I'm your only true love and you're mine. And now we're having a baby together."

"Yes we are. What will we name her?"

"That theory about frequent sex producing a higher percentage of girls is just statistics. We need to pick a girl's name *and* a boy's name. How about Hubert if it's a boy?"

"No way. People would call him Junior, and that would make me think of Tristan's mom. How about Collin?"

"You want to name him after my dad?"

"Sure. It's a good simple name, and I think your dad would love having a grandson named after him."

"And if it's a girl?"

"Your mom was named Sibyl, right? Let's name her after your mom."

"Or we could name her Martha after your mom."

I sat there thinking for a few moments. Sharice asked if something was bothering me.

"I guess it's the uncertainty about my family. I never even thought about these things until Floss Man dropped dead in the Plaza and turned out to share some DNA with me. Maybe we should hold off naming our child after anyone in my family until I know who exactly is in my family."

"Or maybe," she said, "we should forget about family and start afresh. Make up a new name for our child."

"Like Tesla," I said. "I read that over a hundred babies were named after that electric car last year."

"All boys," she ventured.

"You'd think so, but most of them were girls. Maybe their parents wanted to spark a feminist movement in the world of electric cars."

"Groan. I read that religion related names are popular."

"Like Noah or Job?"

"No. Like Halo, Amen, Calvary, and Lucifer."

"Lucifer? Really?"

"Maybe we should just stick to well-known names like Jermajesty."

"Jermajesty is well-known?"

"Of course. The child who was stuck with that name is Jermaine Jackson's son."

"And Jermaine Jackson is?"

"A popular entertainer. No one you'd care about. I went online today and read about names. A New Zealand judge made a 9-year-old child named Talula Does the Hula From Hawaii a ward of the court so she could change her name."

"What kind of parent gives a child a name like that?"

"Immature? Insane? But get this. A court right here in New Mexico last June prevented a man from legally changing his name to *F Censorship*."

She said, "I assume the *f* did not stand for Fred?"

I nodded

Chapter 23

Dean Gangji opened a copy of the *Albuquerque Journal* and read to the assembled department heads.

"As you all know, the State's Attorney General had been investigating UNM. According to the paper, he found 'a disturbing pattern of concealment and deliberate misrepresentation'. According to the report, the AG's Office has investigated 11 complaints about UNM's compliance with the state's Open Meetings Act and Inspection of Public Records Act since 2015. Most of this stems from the use of $25,000 in public funds to pay the expenses of private donors and the attempt to cover up that expenditure by deleting emails and other documents that were subject to the open records law."

He looked up from the paper. "Then there is the other scandal regarding our football coach who was suspended after some players reported being abused and charges that he obstructed a rape investigation and made racist comments. Why do I mention these things?" He held up the 12th day report. "Because they are the primary reason why enrollment is down. Many New Mexicans have lost faith in us. They're not sure they want their sons and daughters here."

His beard seemed to stiffen and his eyes darken. He looked down at the report. "Theater enrollment down eleven percent. Music down seven percent. Communications down four percent. Dance down eight percent."

He looked back up at us. "Waiting for the Board of Regents and the central administration to act is not satisfactory to me. I respect both groups, but I also have responsibility for the College of the Arts. I want a plan on my desk from each of you by Monday morning on how our college can regain the confidence of our stakeholders – our current students, our alumni, public school teachers in our fields, the performing and visual arts institutions around the state, our patrons and donors. And I want concrete steps and timetables."

He stood up and walked out, leaving us sitting in silence.

The guy next to me stuck out his hand and said, "Welcome to the college. I'm Jim Shrader, head of the music department."

I shook his hand and said, "I'm Hubie Schuze, interim head of the art department."

"And off to a great start," he said.

I stared at him blankly.

"Surely you noticed that he didn't mention your enrollment numbers."

"I guess because they're up?"

"Right. He didn't want to soften his tongue lashing of the rest of us by acknowledging any good news. I imagine he'll talk to you about it one-on-one."

And right on cue, Jane Robinson came in the room and said to me, "The dean wants to see you in his office."

~

The walls of Dean Gangji's inner office are decorated with the heads of dead ruminants. I recognize the species native to New Mexico – mountain goats, antelope, deer, and elk. I have seen pictures of the others but am unsure of the names. One I think may be an oryx. Or may *have been* an oryx. It is definitely past tense. I'm a carnivore. So I have few qualms about killing animals in order to eat them. But I don't like seeing their remains on display. Their glass eyes seem to stare at me accusingly.

The same can be said of the dean except for the glass eyes part. But beneath his real eyes his lips form slowly into a smile as he informs me that enrollment in art classes is up seventeen percent.

"16.86," I reply.

He removes a paper from the inner pocket of his suit jacket and glances at it. "Precisely so. And to what do you attribute the increase?"

"First, all three sections of ART 2000 were initially scheduled on the same day at the same time. Rescheduling them on different days and times made it possible for more students to enroll in them. Then I hired an adjunct to teach Digital Art during the day when most students can take it. All the sections were originally scheduled in the evening."

"What else did you do to increase enrollment?"

"I think those two changes account for the enrollment increase."

"There is one more. Surely you noticed in compiling the 12th day report."

I nodded. "Fewer students dropped classes prior to the 12th day. But that is not a result of anything I did."

"On the contrary. By reacting to the needs of students as regards the days and times of course offerings, you demonstrated to them that you care about their success. You have raised student morale."

I thought about the Hawthorn Effect, but said nothing.

"There is one downside to your enrollment increase; namely, your expenditures are higher than the previous semester."

"Actually, they are lower if you compare expenditures to revenue, which is the correct way to measure such things. Last semester, the art department spent $1.39 for every dollar it generated in tuition payments. This semester, we are on course to spend only $1.25 for every tuition dollar we generate."

"But you are spending more on salaries for teachers."

"No. Counting salary and benefits, we gained $107,638 on salary not paid to Milton Shorter and Junior Prather. If you subtract my salary and benefits and those of the three adjuncts I hired, we are actually spending almost $70,000 less than last semester."

His smile disappeared. Maybe I had been too direct or sounded flippant.

"How did you come up with these figures?"

"They're all in the stats sheet Ms. Robinson gave me and online in the Banner software."

"Aren't you a potter? How is it that you are able to handle Banner?"

"I'm not. My nephew gets the figures for me. But I'm the one who analyzes them. My degree from here is actually in accounting."

"How the devil did you end up in the art department?"

"As you said, I'm also a potter."

He relaxed, leaned back in his chair, and laughed. Then he rotated a computer around so that I could see the screen, and he punched a few keys. I watched Stella Ramsey do the summary of her visit with Freddie and his students. The report was as positive as Sharice had claimed it to be.

"You should have told me you were going to hire an ex-convict."

"The handbook for department heads specifies that hiring of adjuncts does not need the approval of the dean's office."

"Correct. But common sense should have told you that consulting the dean in the case of a possibly risky hire would have been prudent."

"I didn't think of it as a risk. I knew what an excellent teacher he is and also that he is a changed man. But I take your point and apologize for not consulting with you in advance."

He nodded and smiled. "Please tell me you are not paying your nephew to manage the Banner software for you."

"I *am* paying him. In cash out of my pocket."

"For the record, you never told me that."

"Never told you what?" I replied, and he smiled.

Chapter 24

"Wow! Congratulations. When's the due date?"

Susannah is not good at curbing her enthusiasm, so everyone in *Dos Hermanas* now knew that Sharice was pregnant. It was a Thursday which meant Sharice was helping Dr. Batres work on poor peoples' teeth.

"Sharice is guessing October."

"Geez, that's almost nine months away. How can she be sure so early?"

"Apparently all you have to do these days is pee on a piece of litmus paper a few minutes after your heart rate slows down from having sex."

"I don't think it's quite that fast. Has she been to a doctor to make sure?"

"Not yet. She's been talking to the staff at work about choosing a doctor. And she also wants to consult with Dr. Rao."

"Why would she want to talk to her cancer doctor?"

"I think she's worried that the effects of her cancer treatment might be grounds for terminating the pregnancy."

"An abortion!"

I nodded.

"You can't let her do that, Hubie."

"I don't like the idea, but it's not my decision. A woman has the right to control her own body."

Her big brown eyes narrowed. "Of course a woman has a right to control her own body. Which means she can get a tattoo on her nose if she wants to or have her appendix removed. But a baby is not part of a woman's body. It has its own body. And its own soul created by God."

I know Susannah and her entire family are devout Catholics, but I was surprised by the zeal of her reaction. So after an awkward pause, I suggested we change the subject.

She took a deep breath then a sip of her margarita. "Sorry, but I feel very strongly about the topic."

"So noted. And I admire you for taking a stand."

She smiled and relaxed. "I've got some news myself," she said, "but it's not as exciting as yours."

"Don't keep me in suspense."

"I know how gurney guy was killed."

"They solved the crime?"

"No. *I* solved it.

What I thought was, *Here we go again*. What I said was, "Okay, give me the solution."

"So you know who John D. MacDonald is, right?"

"Sure. The hamburger guy."

"Sheesh. John D. MacDonald was one the world's greatest murder mystery writers. *Dead Low Tide* was his first great mystery novel. Before that he was just a hack writing science fiction. The protagonist in *Dead Low Tide* is Andy McClintock, an estimator working for a Florida contractor named John Long. Long's wife tells Andy she's worried about her husband and asks Andy to spy on his boss and see what's going on. Andy agrees reluctantly and asks his boss if anything is wrong, which leads to an argument. Andy resigns, but the boss, John, admits something is worrying him. He convinces Andy to stay on and help make sure the current big project is completed. He even gives Andy a raise. Andy is concerned that John may be terminally ill or even suicidal. A night or two later, Andy comes home and surprises an intruder who escapes. Andy searches his place and discovers only one thing is missing."

She stopped talking and stared at me with those big brown eyes.

I obliged her implied request. "What was missing?"

"His harpoon gun. Ta-da!"

"So?"

"It's obvious, Hubie. The key is that a harpoon is attached to a wire so that you can reel in a fish. So the puncture wound in Gurney Guy was caused by a harpoon, and there was no weapon left behind because the harpooner reeled it in and ran off."

"Good theory, but it didn't happen that way. I saw the video. No one was toting a harpoon."

"You tote a six-shooter. You don't tote a harpoon; you carry one."

"If anyone had been carrying one, it would have been reported. After all, harpoons are about as common in New Mexico as bikinis in Greenland."

"Maybe it was a really small harpoon, one you could hide in a hand bag or in the sleeve of a jacket."

"It was unseasonably warm, remember. No one was wearing a jacket."

"Maybe the woman had one in her purse. Was she carrying a purse?"

"I don't remember."

"Ask Whit to let you see the video again."

She looked so dejected that I agreed to ask Whit. I even told her it was a good idea and asked her how things worked out in *Dead Low Tide*.

"The morning after Andy's harpoon was stolen, John is found dead, and the harpoon is sticking in his throat. When the police discover the harpoon belongs to Andy, he becomes a suspect. And then John's wife lies to the police and tells them that she and Andy were having an affair."

"She had set him up right from the start," I said.

"Exactly. And there's also a hastily drawn up contract leaving John Long Contractors to Andy. So he's jailed for killing John Long to get Long's wife and business. We need to find out if Gurney Guy had a wife and a business."

"Yes. But first we have to find out who he is."

She still looked dejected, so I decided to cheer her up with a clue. "While you're thinking about Gurney Guy's demise, throw this into the plot. Whit told me the medical examiner found poison in the wound."

She brightened. "What kind?"

"Palytoxin."

She asked me to spell it.

Chapter 25

Charles Webb was waiting for me at the condo. Sharice had invited him in and given him a coupe of Gruet.

"I told Charles the good news," Sharice said, "and he said that deserved a glass of bubbly."

She handed me one, and Charles handed me the envelope from the Safari Motel.

"What did the DNA test reveal?" I asked.

He had an enigmatic expression I couldn't read. "The hair in this envelope is not from a human."

"Damn. It's from a racoon, right?"

"How did you know?"

"Lucky!"

Now he looked bewildered. "You took a lucky guess and actually got it?"

"No. Lucky is the racoon's name. Tristan's mother keeps him as a pet."

"Is he blind in one eye and recently castrated?"

I laughed and said, "You know that joke, too."

Sharice said, "You sound like a couple of teenagers."

Charles asked why Junior would put racoon hair in a locket and give it to her son.

Sharice said, "If you met her, you would understand."

"Well," he said, "that's not any crazier than my first thought. Which was that someone put racoon hair in there as a racial slur."

"Junior doesn't even know you exist, much less whether you're black or white."

"Hey, I said it was crazy."

Sharice said, "I know *coon* is a racist term in the States for a black person, but I don't understand why. Raccoons have masks and straight hair. We have neither."

"*Coon* doesn't come from raccoon," Charles answered. "It comes from the Spanish word *barracón*."

"Which means what?" Sharice asked.

"A warehouse," I said. "So I'm guessing it's where the captive Africans were kept before being sold and shipped off to the New World."

Charles nodded. "The phrase was popularized in the 19th century by a song titled *Zip Coon*. It was sung in minstrel shows to the tune of Turkey in the Straw:

Old Zip Coon he is a larned skoler,
Sings posum up a gum tree ann conny in a holler.
Posum up a gum tree, coonny on a stump,
Den over dubble trubble, Zip coon will jump.

Then the chorus goes:

O Zip a duden duden duden zip a duden day.
O Zip a duden duden duden duden duden day.
O Zip a duden duden duden zip a duden day.
Zip a duden duden duden zip a duden day.

Does that chorus sound familiar?"

Sharice and I both nodded.

"That's because it was the basis for *Zip-A-Dee-Doo-Dah* in Walt Disney's adaptation of Joel Chandler Harris' Uncle Remus tales, *Song of the South.*"

"So you're saying that *Song of the South* was a racist film?" Sharice asked him.

He shrugged. "That word is so loaded and overused that it's bent out of shape. Racism is a thread through all of human history. So are jealousy and treachery and a lot of other base emotions. We need to strike a balance between recognizing it and not being obsessed with it."

I asked him how we can do that.

He smiled. "Damned if I know."

Chapter 26

The first weeks of the semester had seemed more like September than January – warm days, cool nights, and high blue skies. The only hint of winter was the snow on the Sandias.

The whistling wind woke us before dawn, and we saw snow flying horizontally across the terrace. After I bundled up, I went down to the Bronco, started the engine, and turned on the heater. Then I locked the car and scooted up to the condo ASAP. It takes the old Bronco a long time to get warm, and I planned not to be in at while it was doing so.

Sharice chided me when I came back in. "It's not good for the environment to leave an empty car running."

"Me driving with frozen fingers is potentially even worse for the environment."

She handed me a cup of hot coffee which I used to thaw my hands. We eventually figured out what to wear that would look right for a visit with Consuela and Emilio and also be warm. The Bronco was toasty as we drove down Central to the south valley.

"I remember the first time you took me to meet Consuela, you called her your 'second mom', and I asked if your dad had remarried after your mother died. Now that I know more about him, I can understand why you laughed at the question."

"I can't imagine him ever having eyes for another woman. But the Floss Man enigma has me questioning everything."

She put her left hand gently on my right thigh. "Do you want to continue to help Whit and Charles figure it out, or would it be better if you just let it go? After all, your life is not different just because someone you never knew died and was tied to you genetically."

"You're right. I remember when we came down here last year for Consuela and Emilio's big *Cinco de Mayo* celebration and you had to play the part of the French general who was defeated by the Mexicans."

"Because I speak French."

"Right. But that doesn't make you French any more than my speaking Spanish makes me Mexican. Or Argentinian."

"Or Nicaraguan," she threw in. And we ran through all the countries we could think of where Spanish is widely spoken ending with my mention of The Philippines.

"They still speak Spanish?"

"I think English is now the most widely spoken language there, but Spanish remains common."

"What about their own language?"

"Which of their own languages? There are close to 200 of them."

"It's the same here in New Mexico, isn't it? You told me one time that the main reason the uprisings against the Spanish conquistadors failed was that the First Nations couldn't coordinate their opposition because each tribe had their own language."

'First Nations' is one of the Canadian phrases Sharice retains. At least she doesn't end sentences with 'eh'. That's an anglophone Canadian thing.

~

Despite the freezing weather and high wind, Emilio was outside to greet us as we stepped out of the Bronco. The three of us quick-stepped into the tiny adobe house where we were greeted by Consuela and given a steaming cup of Mexican hot chocolate. Consuela's version is so authentic, I think it must have been handed down to her by the Aztecs. The ingredients are whole milk, cocoa powder, vanilla beans, cinnamon, chili powder, a little bittersweet chocolate, and a few drops of honey. Nothing is better on a cold morning.

After we were all seated, Sharice announced that she was with child. Consuela burst into tears of joy. Emilio retrieved a bottle of Presidente Solera Brandy, added a splash to our cups, and proposed a toast – "May he be the first of many."

Consuela went to their bedroom and emerged with a Mexican *bola,* a traditional chiming pendant worn by expectant mothers during pregnancy. It is worn low to rest directly in front of the baby who will hear the gentle ringing sounds.

"I wore this when I carried Ninfa. Emilio call your baby 'he' because he is macho. But I hope you have a girl."

I said I believed it would be a girl, but I didn't explain why I held that view.

After much discussion of the good news, Emilio suggested he and I move to the kitchen to prepare breakfast while the women "speak of woman things".

We prepared huevos rancheros. Since we'd both been taught to cook by Consuela, we made a good team, and plates were on the table in less than ten minutes. Which was a good thing because the brandy had made its way to my head speeded along by the chili powder and steam.

Consuela, Emilio, and Sharice were doing all the talking. I just listened and ate. And thought about Sharice's suggestion that I forget about Floss Man. Maybe she was right. Sitting in this familiar home was just as warm and reassuring now as it had been over the last thirty years.

When the Basque guy named Shorty disappeared from Otowi, a young San Ildefonso Indian named Adam consented for a while to act as watchman. His parents were Julián and María Martínez—the famous potters. They already owned the land and they bought the house that had been built there.

When Edith Warner replaced Adam as station master, she brought her meagre belongings – a box of books, a barrel of dishes, two cots and four chairs. Church wrote of Edith that, "She found herself thinking of her little German grandmother who as a bereaved and timid young girl had packed her thick Lutheran books in a wooden chest and set sail for a new life in America. It seemed as though the spirits of all women, who since humanity's beginning have made homes in wilderness, came now to companion her like an invisible chorus. Perhaps the trouble with the little house, she thought, was that only rootless men had used it for a shelter. No woman had ever tried to fill it with human warmth and make it beautiful."

I suspected I qualified as a rootless man. I'd spent most of my life sleeping behind my shop. I spent a lot of time at *Dos Hermanas* drinking tequila. I made a living breaking the law. A ridiculous law in my opinion, but men with roots know they are not entitled to choose which laws to obey. But Sharice had taken me in. And now we were having a baby. Being a father made me feel like a man with roots. And I liked it.

When I first used Edith Warner as a source of insight – comparing her taking the job as train stationmaster to my taking the job as department head – it had been mostly in jest, said in order to keep the banter going between myself and Susannah. But as I thought about the way she and Tilano were so different yet so right for each other, how they each made the other's life complete, it was no longer banter. It was a life lesson.

Chapter 27

Sharice had decided to consult her oncologist about choosing an obstetrician.

In plain English, she wanted to ask her cancer doctor about getting a good doctor to deliver a baby. I suspected there was another reason she wanted to see Dr. Rao.

My suspicion was confirmed when Sharice asked Dr. Rao if having been treated for cancer might affect her pregnancy.

Doctor Rao said, "Docetaxel has been shown to be both embryotoxic and foetotoxic in rabbits and rats, and to reduce fertility in rats. As with other cytotoxic medicinal products, docetaxel may cause fetal harm when administered to pregnant women. So I never use docetaxel on a pregnant patient except in very special circumstances. Of course you were not pregnant when you received docetaxel. So the question is whether there are lingering effects. There have been no long-term studies regarding this matter. If you decide to continue the pregnancy, I'd like to meet with your obstetrician so that we can jointly monitor you and the baby."

In addition to the two new words I learned – embryotoxic and foetotoxic – the words that got my attention were, "If you decide to continue the pregnancy."

I didn't want to lose my newfound roots. I didn't want my baby to be denied a chance to experience life. But I also knew even though she would consult me, it would ultimately be Sharice's decision.

The appointment had been scheduled early in the morning and Sharice had been directed to fast because Dr. Rao wanted both blood and urine samples as part of her routine monitoring. After the samples were taken, Dr. Rao said she had called the obstetrician she'd recommend – Dr. Chandra – and scheduled an appointment for tomorrow.

So we headed to The Grove for breakfast. Sharice ordered the organic egg-white frittata with crimini mushrooms, roasted asparagus, tomatoes, and arugula.

To offset all that healthy stuff, I choose the burrito of scrambled egg, Tully's local sausage, goat cheese, and green chile.

After we were seated and our plates delivered, Sharice asked me what I thought.

"The sausage is delicious."

"I meant about what Dr. Rao said."

"I liked the part where she said she wanted to cooperate with Dr. Chandra. And I'm glad she set the appointment up for tomorrow. I'm anxious to hear all about our baby from a doctor who knows that stuff."

"What about what she said about the risk?"

"If I understood correctly, the risk is high if you take it while you're pregnant. But there's no data on whether there's a risk years after you've taken it. You're a health professional. Would traces of it still be in your system?"

"I doubt it. But it's effects could linger."

"What sort of effects?"

"I have no idea. But there are certain medicines that weaken teeth. Years afterwards, there is no evidence of the medicine in the body, but the weakened teeth remain a problem. Maybe the docetaxel could have affected the ability of my body to develop a healthy umbilical cord."

I guess I frowned because she added, "It's just an example."

"And there are other possibilities, so that's why it's good that you're meeting with Doctor Chandra tomorrow. You can ask her lots of questions."

"What if she doesn't have any answers?"

Chapter 28

William Hughes, Assistant Director of the Office of Compliance, showed up again Tuesday morning in my office to tell me the complaint he had told me about had been dropped and asked me if I had talked to Professor Armstrong, insinuating – it seemed to me – that I might have coerced Armstrong into dropping the complaint.

"I have not spoken to him since your last visit. I haven't even seen him. And anyway, you never told me that he was the person who made the complaint. I was just guessing."

"We have to protect complainants from retaliation, and the best way is to keep their identity unknown until the formal process begins."

"That makes sense."

He smiled. It looked like something he rarely did.

Then he frowned and said, "Another complaint has been filed against you, this time anonymously, so I couldn't tell you who filed it even if I wanted to. The complaint charges that you violated Physical Plant Regulation 107r which prohibits 'defacing or destroying buildings and/or equipment belonging to the University'. Specifically, it claims that you defaced or caused to be defaced the door to one of the faculty offices."

Obviously the door to Bakke's office. But she was happy with the change. I couldn't imagine who might have complained about changing the way the door opened, but at least I had a defense against the charge.

"I did have a change made to the door to a faculty office, but it was not defaced."

"Perhaps in your opinion it was not defaced, but the regulation defines *defacing* as 'any alteration that changes the function or appearance of the building or object'."

I ask Mr. Hughes to follow me to Bakke's office. I pointed to the door. "The change to that door is an artwork," I said.

"An artwork?"

"Yes. A class project by the students in Professor Olley's class in wood sculpturing. It was approved by me and overseen by the professor."

"How does changing its hinges make a door become a work of art?"

"How does displaying a picture of a can of soup become a work art? Art can be anything these days. And if you try to change it back, you'll likely be charged with censorship."

He looked at me apprehensively.

"Think about the *The Three Cultures* mural in the library," I said. "You want to get caught up in something like that?"

He shook his head slowly. For once I thought he and I agreed about something. After a few moments of reflection, he said, "I'll discuss it with my supervisor. Maybe she'll agree with the art angle and let it go."

"You are obviously knowledgeable about all the rules and regulations around here," I said. "Is it possible for me to see my father's personnel file?"

"Is your father a UNM employee?"

"He was. He taught here for many years before he retired and eventually died."

"Are you his heir?"

"Yes. His only heir."

"Then you are entitled to see the files and receive copies of any or all of the contents. However, the university is allowed to charge you for the cost of making copies if they choose to do so."

I thanked him for the information, and he left.

~

Freddie came by before his class and asked, "Do you know what's going on with *The Three Cultures Mural* in the library? They have a curtain over it. If there's a restoration project for it, I'd love to be involved as an artist."

"They aren't restoring it; they're hiding it."

"Why?"

"Some people think it's racially insensitive because the Hispanic guy looks like a laborer, the Indian guy looks like an artisan, and the white guy is in the middle and above them."

Freddie's brow furrowed. "It was painted during the depression as a WPA project or something as I recall. It probably provided work for Hispanics, Native Americans, and Anglos when jobs were scarce. And what's wrong with being a laborer or artisan? Hell, you and I are artisans."

I shrugged. "These days anything that anyone finds offensive has to be knocked down or painted over."

"That's censorship! Every art work ever created offends someone or depicts something someone dislikes. Diego Rivera was Hispanic. But his painting *Flower Festival* has the Native American women shown only from behind. But we see the faces of the Europeans in the picture. That was also painted in the 1930s and sends the message that the native people were not as important as the Europeans, which at that point was the accepted view. It's not right ethically. But it's historically accurate. Should we tear down the coliseum in Rome because people were fed to lions or gladiators were forces to fight to the death? If you get rid of all negative things in history, there won't be much history left."

"History isn't very popular these days."

"Who said, 'Those who cannot remember their past are condemned to repeat it'?"

"George Santayana. Full name, Jorge Agustín Nicolás Ruiz de Santayana y Borrás."

Freddie laughed and said, "Now that is Hispanic!"

"Your reaction to the mural issue is mild compared to Susannah's."

He brightened. "What did she say?"

"That anyone whose psyche is so fragile that it's offended by a hundred-year-old mural needs to get three things - a job, a life, and a backbone."

"Sounds like her. Working a ranch has put a lot of spunk in that woman."

His eyes moistened.

"Don't give up hope," I said.

"I'll never do that." He was silent for a moment then said, "The main reason I came by was to thank you for arranging for Stella Ramsey to publicize me teaching a class."

"No need to thank me. In fact, I benefitted from it more than you did. Dean Gangji was unhappy about me hiring an ex con. But the publicity was so good that he decided to let it go."

"I'm happy for you. But you're wrong in thinking it benefitted you more than me. I received a benefit you don't know about."

He was smiling like the cat who ate a – forget the canary – make it a turkey, complete with gravy and cranberry sauce. "Was this extra benefit one of the things you listed as what you most missed while in prison?"

He was astonished. "How did you guess?"

"Your list was freedom, sex, and booze. You earned your freedom. I bought you a drink, and Stella has a thing about men who seem down and out."

"Did you expect I would end up in her bed?"

"No. But if the idea had crossed my mind, I would have thought it not unlikely. So what now?"

"I'd give her up in a heartbeat just to have lunch with Susannah."

~

Melvin Armstrong arrived moments later. He skipped the nicety of a greeting and said, "I need a new kiln."

"Is something wrong with the current one?"

"No. I want a different type, a raku kiln. I don't suppose you know what that is."

"I'm a potter. Why would you think I don't know what a raku kiln is?"

"Because you just copy Native American stuff."

A reasonable answer.

"How much does the kiln cost?"

"A little over $2,000 with shipping."

"Okay. Get me the details, and I'll process a purchase order."

He stared at me. "That's it?"

"Yes. I think all I need for the purchase order is the item number, description, price, and vendor."

"I don't have to make a formal request?"

"No. Verbal is fine."

"Why are you doing this?"

"If you asked me for a block of granite to carve a statue, I might need more of an explanation. But you teach ceramics. And you said you need a raku kiln. And there's enough money in the budget to buy one. So that's what we'll do."

"Good," he said and walked away.

~

William Hughes returned a while later and handed me a box. "This is your father's complete personnel file."

I took the box from him and felt its heft. "Looks like I'm going to have a gigantic copying charge."

"No charge at all. The people in the HR department were happy to get rid of it."

"Don't they need it for historical purposes?"

"All those old files were digitized several years ago."

I smiled at what my father might have said

about his files being digitized.

"I hope you won't mind that I looked through the files," he said. "I have the right to do so, but I feel the need to tell you that I looked."

"And?"

"Your father had a distinguished career. You should be proud of him."

"I am."

~

I spent the rest of the day reading about my father.

Chapter 29

Silver City is nestled on the south side of the Gila Wilderness, the world's first wilderness area, so designated on June 3, 1924.

Some would say the south valley of Albuquerque is a wilderness. So what does 'wilderness' mean in the case of the Gila? According to federal regs, it means no motorized or mechanized vehicles, including bicycles. Camping and fishing are allowed with proper permit, but no roads, buildings, logging, or mining are permitted.

The Gila Wilderness is named after the Gila River, and the beds of its several branches are the lowest elevations in the wilderness, just below 5000 feet. The Mogollon Mountains arc across the wilderness, the highest point being Whitewater Baldy at 11,000 feet.

The Mimbres people lived in the area between 1000 and 1130 AD, and they left many cliff dwellings and other evidence of their culture. The 'other evidence' is mainly pottery. And I have dug up and copied some of it.

My second favorite thing about the Gila Wilderness, after the pottery, is the white-nosed coati mundi. And I remain steadfast in my admiration for this species despite having been bitten by one of them. Which is a lot less serious than being bitten by the animal that bears the wilderness's name – the Gila monster. Their venom is highly poisonous.

Sharice awoke from a brief nap along I - 25 South and said, "Why would your father take a sabbatical in Silver City?"

"Junior told us he'd been on sabbatical when I was born, but she was mistaken. Not about the year. But she was mistaken about the sabbatical part. I found out by reading his personnel files that it was a leave without pay."

"That makes even less sense."

"Exactly. Which is why I decided to go there and see if I can find out anything about why he was there and what he did. There's a good little university there – Western New Mexico University. But it's not the sort of place to attract researchers like my father. He had been to Silver City many times because there was a Veterans Hospital at Fort Bayard just a few miles from town."

"Was he in bad health?"

"He turned 18 in 1944, at which time he enlisted in the Navy and served in the Pacific. He came back with tuberculosis and received treatment at Fort Bayard."

"Maybe that's all it was in 1969 – a hospital stay."

"No. He was cured long before I was born.

The hospital was eventually closed, but I don't know exactly when. What I do know is that he came to know the area well, and he liked it."

Sharice asked why I was laughing.

"I was just remembering one of dad's favorite stories about Patsy Miller, a nurse at the hospital. He took treatment there and then did yearly check-ups until the late fifties. Dad used to tell us he could hear the clack of her shoes as she walked down the hall to give the patients their shots while they joked, 'Roll over! Target practice time!' So he didn't go there in 1969 for health reasons. And if he was doing research, he would have had a sabbatical or at least received his pay and possibly some stipend."

"How can you find out anything after fifty years, especially since there was no official reason for his visit? If he just rented a hotel room and took an extended vacation, no one's going to remember him after fifty years."

"I have an informant."

"Who is it?"

"Sin Po."

"Must be related to Faye Po."

Faye Po is a lady of Chinese ancestry and one of my best customers. I told Sharice that Sin Po was Faye Po's brother.

"Is he old enough to remember anything about your father?"

I nodded. "Faye Po is 96. Sin is 97. He was

around my age when my father was there."

"What was a Chinaman doing in Silver City?"

I laughed. "They had a Chinatown. Not as big as the one in San Francisco in terms of numbers, but probably about the same in terms of percentages. Many of the gold rush towns had Chinese residents."

"They were miners?"

"Some were. But most of them started as domestic workers – maids, stable hands, gardeners, etc. They saved their money and then opened restaurants, grocery stores, laundries, and such."

"Which one did Sin Po open?"

"A restaurant. It's closed now, but it operated for many years. My father loved Chinese food, so I'm betting he ate there."

"And you think Sin Po will remember him after all these years."

"You met Faye Po. Remember her talking about her childhood in China? If her brother's memory is half as good as hers, he'll remember."

~

Other than by airplane, helicopter or rocket, there is no direct route from Albuquerque to Silver City. You have to skirt the Gila Wilderness on the east or west side. I chose the east. Even though it's mostly freeway, the last segment is a beautiful ride across the mountains from Truth or Consequences to Silver City.

Sin Po lived in a turn-of-the-century cottage four blocks from the Palace Hotel where we had a reservation. We checked in, rested from the drive, freshened up and rang his doorbell a little after 3:00 pm.

I told him who I was and introduced Sharice.

"You look like your picture," he said to her.

"Where did you see her picture?" I asked.

"Facebook. Dr. Batres has business page with pictures of staff. Please come inside. Is very cold on porch."

Sin Po had a pleasant countenance and very few wrinkles for a man of his age, mainly laugh lines by his eyes and a few shallow furrows across his brow. His eyes were like the stars on a clear desert night – big and bright.

The walls of the small living room were covered with family photos, including many of Faye Po at different ages.

I handed him two packages and said, "The *Lai-See* [lucky money] envelope is from your sister. The box is from me."

He thanked me, put the *lisee* envelope in his pocket, opened the box and thanked me for the Al Azar cherry wine produced by the Don Quixote Distillery in Los Alamos. His sister had told me he enjoys a small glass of it after his evening meal.

"Faye told me you are curious about your father's stay here many years ago."

"Yes. It was from December of 1968 until June of 1969. He and my mother liked Chinese food, so I imagine they must have dined in your restaurant."

"He was a college professor?"

"Yes."

"How tall was he?"

"Taller than me," I said and we all laughed. "He was about five or six inches taller than I am."

"Did he teach history?" he asked.

Yes!, I thought. *He does remember him*. "Yes, he taught mainly history of the southwest."

"Your mother was quite striking because she was so tall and thin."

"Yes, she was always thin but not in an unhealthy way. Of course she wouldn't have been thin when they were here because she was pregnant."

"Oh. Then perhaps the couple I remember were not your parents. The woman was definitely not with child. That I am sure of."

"Do you remember their names?" I asked hopefully.

He shook his head. "I remember them because they came often and he was a professor of history. But I do not know if I ever knew their family name or first names."

"Does the name *Schuze* sound familiar?"

"No. Was it a nickname perhaps?"

"No. It's spelled S-c-h-u-z-e. Not like footwear."

"Ah."

"What about Martha or Lawton?"

"No. Sorry. I knew more customers by their faces than by their names. Do you have pictures?"

I shook my head. The only photos of my parents that were in their house after they died were from a Polaroid camera. As you probably remember, they made instant photos. But after many years, those instant photos were faded beyond recognition.

Another failure of high tech, I thought to myself. The drawings on the cliff dwellings north of town are a thousand years old, and you can tell exactly what they are.

~

We took Mr. Po to dinner. Sharice said it was a nice place and the food was terrific. I don't recall either. The only thing I recall was Mr. Po telling us that his father was so cheap that he would get to work in the morning by depressing the clutch of his 1948 Packard and coasting downhill to save gasoline.

Back at the hotel, she asked why I was so distracted at the restaurant.

"I was thinking about two scenarios. The first is that the couple he remembered were not my parents. The second one, and the one I think must be the case, is that they *were* my parents, and they adopted me. That's why my mother was not pregnant. They came here to adopt a child because they didn't want anyone in Albuquerque to know it was not their biological child."

"Why?"

"Because they thought I might feel bad about being adopted. Lots of people used to adopt children and never tell the kids they were adopted. So my parents wanted to make sure no one in Albuquerque knew. Because if anyone did, he or she might accidentally let it slip."

"Why would they come to Silver City to adopt a child? Is there an orphanage here or something?"

"There's no orphanage so far as I know. I think they came here because my father knew a lot of people here from his visits during the fifties. They were mostly health care workers. They probably knew he had no children, and he may have mentioned that he would like to. If a pregnant woman told her doctor she wanted to give up the child after it was born, the close-knit health worker community here would have known about it. I'm thinking one of them contacted my father. Then my parents told everyone they were expecting a child and were taking a leave without pay to concentrate on the pregnancy. Since their friends would likely have known they'd been wanting a child for a long time, taking time off to concentrate on the pregnancy would not have seemed odd."

Sharice said, "I think the first scenario is just as likely. The man Sin told us about could have been a professor here at Western New Mexico University. He taught here for a year, got a better job and moved on. After all, history is a common subject. Every university has a bunch of history profs. It's not like your dad taught particle physics or Korean literature."

"True. And you know what? It doesn't matter. Because the other thing I was working through in my mind while you were devouring the Cantonese tamale was that the adoption theory is the only plausible explanation of my being a close relative of Floss Man. He had the same biological as I did."

"And it doesn't bother you to learn you may have been adopted?"

"It's a big surprise, but not a negative one. It's a lot better than finding out one of my parents had an affair that led to an illegitimate child. And the upbringing I had would not have been any different had I been their biological child."

"That makes sense, but still... I mean... it

doesn't bother you at all?"

"Actually," I joked, "I find being adopted a great relief. It explains Floss Man. It explains why I'm shorter than both my parents. And it will save me a lot of time when I go to a new doctor of some sort and they ask me to fill out one of those forms where they ask you if anyone in your family has ever suffered from heart disease, diabetes, tuberculosis, or leprosy."

She laughed and said she thought leprosy was not listed on those forms. Then she said, "But what if you aren't adopted?"

"It doesn't matter. Call it a hypothesis. I choose it because it fits the facts I have. I can't prove it now. Maybe I never can. In that sense it's like Fermat's last theorem"

"Who is Fermat and what is his last theorem?"

"Fermat was a French mathematician who put forth the theorem that says the Pythagorean Theorem has no whole number solutions for any exponent larger than 2."

She frowned and asked for an explanation.

"Almost everyone in the world has learned the Pythagorean Theorem, most of them against their wishes. It says that in any right triangle, the square of the hypotenuse is equal to the sum of the squares of the other two sides, or $c^2 = a^2 + b^2$. If you put a higher exponent like 3, the equation would be $a^3 + b^3 = c^3$. And no matter what whole numbers you assign to A, B, and C, the equation never works. So that's Fermat's Theorem. Stated generally, it says that for the equation $a^x + b^x = c^x$, there are no whole number solutions if X is greater than 2."

"I vaguely remember this stuff from high school. But why bring it up now?"

"Because Fermat wrote in the margin of a book that he had proved it. And he said there was not enough room in the margin to write down the proof. But after over 300 years, no one could figure out a proof. So they eventually decided that either he was playing a joke on posterity or had simply made a mistake. But regardless of that, all mathematicians believe the theorem is true. So I believe I am adopted even though I can't yet prove it."

"Do you want to prove it? Do you want to be sure?"

"It would be nice. But not necessary. And how would I prove it? Put an ad in the Silver City newspaper, 'Seeking local woman who gave up baby for adoption in 1969'?"

"Maybe you just go the records office here and ask if they have a record of your birth."

~

I thought about Sharice's suggestion most of the night. At first I was inclined to just forget it. Treat it like Fermat's theorem and move on. Then I began to inch towards thinking, *what harm can it do*? Drop by the records office, ask about birth records, and maybe find out for sure if I'm adopted.

I finally fell asleep around 2:00. I woke up at 7:00 to the sound of a horse clopping down Main Street. I went to the window because I was wondering if it really was a horse, and it was. Complete with a rider wearing blue jeans, boots, chaps, a fleece-lined leather jacket, a beat-up cowboy hat and a smile. He spotted me at the window, touched two fingers to the brim of his hat, and kept riding.

Silver City is that type of place. A combination of ranchers, farmers, miners, aging hippies, artists, college students, Mexican-Americans, veterans in bad health but good spirits, back-to-earthers, and retirees.

The place has always been laid back. A flood in 1895 washed away the main street. The town responded by relocating the main street to the other side of the buildings, and making their back doors their front doors. The former main street is now called The Big Ditch and serves as a combination nature preserve and park.

The records office is on Copper Street near the intersection with Broadway, just a few steps from the Palace. I was greeted by Sharon Maddus, a harried-looking woman with dark circles under her eyes. She apologized for being disorganized, saying she was a single mom with three kids at home she had to get ready for school before coming to work. Then she explained that New Mexico law specifies that birth records become public records 100 years after the date of birth while death records become public records 50 years after the date of death.

I smiled at her and said, "In that case, I don't think you can help me. I was interested in my own birth record, but I doubt I'll be here fifty years from now when it becomes public."

She smiled back and said, "So you are fifty? You don't look it." She straightened her hair and tried to smile. I think she was flirting with me. Probably needed someone to help with the kids. Being short and older than her wouldn't disqualify me.

"Thanks. I'm actually 49, but I'll hit fifty in a bit over 3 months. I think I was born here, but I'm not certain."

"Why are you uncertain of your place of birth?"

"It's a long story."

She shrugged the sort of shrug that says *I don't need to hear a long story*. Then she said, "No one other than you or someone you designate can get your birth record because it isn't yet public. But you can get it."

"I think I may have been adopted."

"Ah. Well that makes it more complicated.

Because other people are involved such as the birth mother and father, New Mexico adoption records become sealed after the completion of all adoption proceedings. The state does have a program called the Confidential Intermediary Search Program. Adopted adults age 18 or older, adoptive parents of an adoptee under 18, birth parents, or birth siblings may petition the court to hire a confidential intermediary. If the adopted adult or birth parents are deceased or cannot be contacted, the court will decide whether to release the identifying information. Would you like a copy of the form used to petition for a Confidential Intermediary Search?"

"No. But thanks for the explanation and your help."

~

When I returned to the Palace to check out, Sharice told me Sin Po had dropped by to tell her something he had forgotten. On a couple of visits to his restaurant, the history professor and his wife had been accompanied by a young woman who was pregnant.

"That cinches it," I said.

On the road to Hatch, I told Sharice about my visit to the records office, and she asked why I had decided not to ask for a Confidential Intermediary Search.

"Because it's like poking at a hornets' nest.

Assume I am adopted. Do you think my birth mother – the young pregnant girl Sin Po remembers – wants it known that she had a baby and gave it up for adoption? Maybe she got married a year or two later and never told her husband about the baby. And then out of the blue it becomes public. It just doesn't seem right."

We stopped at Hatch and bought two five-pound bags of green chile. One for me and one for Consuela and Emilio. Then we made the boring drive north from Hatch to Albuquerque on I - 25.

We stopped briefly to deliver the green chile to Consuela and Emilio. They insisted we stay for a cup of coffee which we did. Then I asked to go to their bathroom.

Go to the bathroom. It's a euphemism. What we want is not literally to *go* to the bathroom. Bathrooms are seldom so interesting that you want to visit them just to take a look to them. What you actually want to do is answer the call of nature. But in this case, I was not being called.

Chapter 30

Susannah stared at me over the *Dos Hermanas* tiled table and said, "I was so mad at you for not having a cell phone. But when I calmed down, I realized it was actually better that you didn't have one. It would be a lot more fun to give you this news in person."

"Great. So give it to me."

"I solved the mystery of Gurney Guy."

I opened my mouth to say something but she cut me off. "Don't give me one of your condescending 'Great! Tell me about it' replies. This time I gave the info to Whit and he acted on it."

"Great! Tell me about it."

"Groan. You are terrible, you know that?"

"Sure. That's why we're best friends."

She shook her head and continued. "The key was palytoxin."

"I've heard that word before."

"Right. When you spoke it to me."

"I spoke it to you?"

"Yes. When you told me Whit said the lab guys had found it in Gurney Guy's wound."

I nodded.

She said, "I looked it up on the internet. It's produced by a zoanthid, a small marine animal related to sea anemones and corals. But not all zoanthids produce it. Only a few living in certain tidal pools make it, and most of them are in Hawaii. A version of it extracted from zoanthids in a tidal pool off Maui is the most potent variety. So while browsing websites having to do with Hawaii, I ran across something called a Hawaiian sling. It's a very small version of a harpoon. Remember I mentioned that a harpoon may have been the weapon?"

I nodded.

"Since the poison was likely from Hawaii, and the Hawaiian sling is a small harpoon that can be concealed in a purse, I figured I was on the right track. So I searched the missing persons list in Hawaii and found an article about a prominent former citizen of Hilo who disappeared. And the pictures of him in the newspapers looked a bit like you. I turned my research results over to Whit who contacted the Hawaiian authorities. And guess what?"

I was numb. I just turned up my palms.

"They got an exact match. Gurney Guy is the missing Hawaiian."

"And he's related to me?"

"Must be."

"But how?"

"I don't know. But now that we know who he is, it should be easy to connect the dots."

"What if I don't want the dots connected?"

"Too late. This is a murder investigation. They aren't going to stop looking for the murderer just because you don't want to know who Gurney Guy is."

We talked a bit more. Actually, she did most of the talking. I was in a stupor. We finished our Margaritas. It was freezing outside. She put on her puffy jacket, and I put on my handmade horsehide jacket. We were about halfway across the Plaza when I felt something hit my lower back.

"Ouch!"

"What's wrong?"

"I think some kid threw a rock at me. I felt it hit my back."

Susannah jerked up my jacket and shirt and looked at my lower back. "It didn't penetrate, but take that coat off carefully and do it now. And call the cops!" she added as she raced away.

I've found it's best always to do what Susannah asks, so I scurried back to Spirits in Clay and dialed 911.

The Plaza was pristine. When it gets real cold in Albuquerque, it also gets quiet, like the air is too thick to convey sound waves. But the sirens were loud enough. And when I pointed the cops in the right direction, they sprinted away and found Susannah standing over the trussed body of a woman.

Remember I said she can ride horses, rope goats, and castrate calves? She had employed that middle skill to truss up my assailant with the line from the Hawaiian sling that she had fired at me.

Chapter 31

Susannah, Charles, and I were in Whit's office.

Whit said, "You called him the dead guy, Gurney Guy and Floss Man. His real name was Frank Wilde. His father was Garner Wilde who attended Western New Mexico University in the late sixties on a basketball scholarship. Like you, Hubert, he was short. But unlike you, he was athletic. Led his high school team to the Hawaii state championship. But being as how he was short, the only school that offered him an athletic scholarship was Western."

Susannah said, "How would Western even know about him as a high school kid in Hawaii?"

Whit said, "Western back then was in the Pacific West Conference. One of the other schools in that conference was The University of Hawaii at Hilo. So the basketball team at Western travelled to Hilo every year, and coaches are always looking for talent."

"I didn't even know Western played sports," I said. "And I thought The University of Hawaii was in Mānoa."

"That's the big campus," Whit said. "They play in the same conference as the Lobos. The little Hawaii campus at Hilo plays in Division 2.

Nobody knows much about them because they ain't on TV. Of course you don't know that 'cause you don't have a TV."

"And wouldn't watch sports if I did."

"Can we get back to the murder?" asked Susannah

Charles said, "While Garner was at Western, he fathered a child with a local girl. Then he went back to Hawaii and made a fortune in fish futures."

"What are fish futures?"

Charles said, "A form of commodity trading. He would speculate about fish prices based on fishing conditions and then buy or sell them before they were even caught."

"Anyway," said Whit, "Garner had two other children in addition to you, Frank and Bette. You already know how they're related to you."

"Half siblings," I said.

"Right. And they were his only heirs because his wife died in an auto accident when the children were very young. What we don't know is the identity of your birth mother."

I nodded.

"The woman we got in custody thanks to Miss Inchaustigui is Bette Wilde. She's the one who killed her brother."

"Why?"

"Speculation at this point," said Charles,

"but agents in Hawaii have been interviewing people, and we think we have it pieced together. Like Whit said, Garner became extremely wealthy. His two legitimate children took divergent paths. Frank enjoyed being the son of a rich man. He attended private schools, took a degree in Italian literature at Stanford, lived in Hilo but spent a lot of time in Florence, Italy. Bette became a playgirl, got into drugs and would have gone to jail had her father not had money and contacts. As far as we can determine, her only job skill was pickpocketing. I say that because she was arrested for it three times and, as in the drug charges, her father managed to keep her out of prison, although she did spend a few weeks in jail. She was basically waiting for her father to die so that she could get her inheritance, which – according to people who knew her – she would have burned through in a year or two. Garner Wilde died in November. His will left a third of his fortune to – and I quote – 'the child I fathered in New Mexico if he or she is still alive and can be located'. We have a long chain of emails between Bette and Frank after their father died. She argued they had no reason to go looking for a lost heir. Frank said they had to honor the will. She tried to change his mind but finally appeared to give up. No more emails until December when Frank told Bette he had hired a private eye to track down the missing half-sibling, and the detective had located him in Albuquerque. Bette agreed to meet him in Albuquerque so they could both meet you, Hubie, and tell you the good news. Evidently, her plan was to prevent you from ever finding out."

I looked at Charles then at Whit. "How would a private eye be able to figure out something neither the Albuquerque Police nor the FBI could figure out?"

Whit bristled slightly at the implied insult, but Charles answered. "First off, he knew the unknown child had been conceived in Silver City. Something we had no way of knowing at that point. Second, a private eye can get certain info more easily because he or she doesn't have to follow any rules. Because New Mexico adoption records are sealed, even the FBI would have to go to court to try and gain access. But a private eye can just bribe a clerk or even break into the records office at night."

I thought back to Ms. Maddus at the Silver City records office. I didn't like to insult her even if only in my own mind, but I wondered if she might have given me a copy of my birth records in exchange for a crisp hundred dollar bill.

I looked at Susannah. "You really did solve this murder."

"I did."

"So why would Bette use such an odd weapon?"

Susannah said, "Easy. She came here from Hawaii. You can't stick a gun in the trunk of your pickup and drive to the mainland. But you can pack a vial with less than 3.5 ounces of poison and the components of a Hawaiian sling in a suitcase and it'll all pass right through security. Then after she was here, all she had to do was sharpen the stick and dip it into the poison."

"And it's just coincidence that she and her brother were in the Old Town Plaza at the same time?"

"How many times have I told you there are no coincidences in murders? She agreed to go with Frank to give you the news. Then, as they were walking across the Plaza, she said her shoe was untied or her panties were riding up or some other excuse to drop back a few paces. Then she pulls the sling from her purse and lets fly."

"Why didn't we see it on the video?"

"She probably activated the Hawaiian sling just before the video started. She may have been just finishing reeling it in as we see him stumble. But because she is behind him, we don't see her in full until he falls."

Charles said, "Seems obvious that Bette killed Frank to prevent you from getting a share of the inheritance. And she almost killed you. It will take a long time to sort all this out. But it looks like you might end up with the entire estate. Bette will get nothing if she is found guilty of murdering Frank because a felon cannot benefit from a crime. Frank can't inherit because he's deceased and has no heirs and no will."

"I think there may be another person related to me who should get a share," I said.

They all stared at me.

I handed an envelope to Charles. "One more DNA test, please."

Then I asked Whit if the pot shard he found in Frank's pocket was evidence.

"Nah," he said, "It's got nothing to do with his murder. You want it?"

I said I did, and he gave it to me.

Chapter 32

I walked west on Central then turned north onto the Rio Grande levee and walked a couple of miles sorting out thoughts and emotions. There's something timeless and soothing about the river. I remembered another thing Edith Warner wrote: "My friend was wrong who said that this country was so old it does not matter what we Anglos do here. What we do anywhere matters but especially here. It matters very much. Mesas and mountains, rivers and trees, winds and rains are as sensitive to the actions and thought of humans as we are to their forces. They take into themselves what we give off and give it out again."

Thinking about myself as part of the eco-system, so to speak, made individual genetics seem a lot less important. I walked back downtown to the condo and told Sharice the entire story.

The next morning, we went to see Father Groas, the priest at St. Neri Catholic Church in Old Town. I consider him to be my spiritual advisor.

I don't know what he considers me to be. Probably the weird misfit who seeks his advice.

He greeted us in his Eastern European

accent. "Gude marning, Youbird and Sharize. To what do I owe the plahsure of you visit?" He sounds like a refugee from the Cold War.

"Sharice has consented to marry me. We'd like you to perform the ceremony."

"Congratulations, Youbird. I wooed be happy to do so. Do you booth plan to convert to Catholicism?"

We declined the offer and reminded him I'm a backslid Episcopalian and Sharice was raised in the same denomination, but she refers to it as 'Anglican'.

Father Groas smiled again and said, "Catholic Light. Very close, but we cannot use the church for the wedding."

"How about the gazebo in the Plaza?"

"Pearfect."

We went to the courthouse and got a license. I dropped Sharice off at work since she was already late, lunchtime actually.

I bought a dozen sunflowers. I went to Treasure House and asked John to recommend a murder mystery. He handed me a copy of *Herbie's Game* by Tim Hallinan.

"This book won the Lefty for best mystery a few years back. If you've finally decided to read a murder mystery, this is a great one to start with."

"I don't plan to read it. It's a gift for Susannah."

"She'll love it. And I know she hasn't read it because she buys her mysteries here."

I went to La Placita and gave the flowers and book to Susannah.

"What's the occasion?"

"Just thanking you for chasing down my assailant. And for being a friend all these years. And also apologizing for making fun of your theory that murder mysteries reflect real life. I was wrong. Your murder mystery reading actually solved a real murder."

"I love Hallinan's books. His protagonist – Junior Bender – says burglaries have to be planned backwards."

"What does that mean?

"It means the first thing you plan is the last thing you do; namely, getting out of the place you burgled. You should keep that in mind."

"I'm not a burglar."

"So you always say. But you've broken into lots of places."

"Always with good reason."

"Another thing you always say."

"Here's something I don't say often enough. I love you, Susannah,"

"I know." She hugged me and kissed me on the cheek. "I love you too, Hubie."

~

I returned to my closet office and read from Peggy Pond Church's book.

~

When Edith told Tilano that she came from Philadelphia his eyes had lighted up. "Philadelphia!" he said. "I've been there. When I came back from Europe, I stopped in Philadelphia for a while. Then I came home to the pueblo." With only a little coaxing he unfolded the story she was to hear so often. A group of Indians from San Ildefonso had gone to Coney Island one summer to display their dances. There Bostok, the animal trainer, had seen them and asked them to go with him on tour. "Paris was the best place," Tilano said. "We stayed there a long time—maybe a month or more. The people liked us and clapped lots when we came out on the stage. When we walked on the street, they crowded around us and asked, 'Are you American Indians?' Soon we learned some words of their language and could answer them. I do not know exactly when it was that Tilano came to live permanently at the little house. In his own way he was as much alone as Edith. His wife had died in childbirth, in the second year of their marriage. What wonder that she at last suggested that he come and live there instead of driving to and from his daily tasks across the bridge? What wonder that he agreed to come, saying only, "You need a man to help you."

~

The story comforts me.

Charles arrives.

"The hair you gave me is from your birth mother, right?"

"Right."

"The DNA is consistent with that. Anything else you need?"

"No."

Tears are coming down my cheeks. He puts his big hand on my shoulder. "Anything I can do?"

I shake my head.

He says, "My father taught me that a man should always be guided by the three M's – morals, mind, and muscle. In that order. You might want to give it some thought as you decide what to do."

I nod. He leaves. He doesn't ask who my birth mother is. Maybe he knows the hair came from the brush in the bathroom at the small adobe in the south valley where I went to the bathroom for the purpose of finding it. He usually knows everything.

Maybe not this time.

Chapter 33

Maybe it was Charles Webbe saying a private detective could "break into the records office at night." Or maybe it was Susannah telling me that Junior Bender planned burglaries backwards.

More likely it was the combination of both that made me decide to break in to the records office in Silver City. And I did start with a plan of how to get out of the place after I got the two things I came for – my birth records and verification of what I thought I knew.

The exit plan was simple – wait until Sharon Maddus opened in the morning and then just walk out the unlocked door when she was back among the files. Her disorganized approach to her duties made the plan virtually foolproof.

The same could not be said about getting in. My only burglaring skill – loiding a spring lock – is useless in the presence of the dual cylinder deadbolt on the front door. So I waited until Maddus was in the back and entered as silently as possible late in the afternoon, my shoes in my backpack. I padded across the room and into the men's room.

I heard Ms. Maddus lock up at five. But I remained in the men's room until midnight, at which time I was confident Copper Street would be dark and deserted. I found my way to the files and begin searching.

It took only twenty minutes to find the cabinets with the birth records. It took over two hours to find mine. Searching the files was exasperating because I was using a penlight. I held it in my mouth because it took both hands to open the files.

The organization of the files was even more exasperating. As I expected, they were organized by date. But nothing was listed on my birthday. A baby dubbed Ronnie B. Harvey by his parents was born on May 4, 1969. Maybe the middle initial stood for 'Big'; he was a whopping eight and a half pounds. David R. Blanco was born on May 6, 1969, roughly a pound and a half lighter than Ronnie. No one was born on my birthday, May 5. At least not in Silver City.

My first thought was a filing error. So I searched all of May, 1969. Didn't take that long, and didn't yield any record of me being born. So I did the whole damn year of 1969. Still no me.

I thought about all the files. I took one out at random and read it all the way from top to bottom. Several times. Until I finally focused on one of the entries on the form: 'Father's name'. I went through all the 1969 records again. Every baby had a father listed.

But my father might not have been listed. The wording of his will – "the child I fathered in New Mexico if he or she is still alive" – showed he wasn't there when I was born. Maybe the 'Father's name' field on my record was blank or read 'unknown'.

So I started looking in different cabinets until I finally located the records of births where the baby had been put up for adoption. We were segregated from the babies from traditional married couples. Probably because our records are confidential. As you would expect, there weren't many of us. I was one of only three in 1969. The 'Father's name' field on my record was not blank as I had guessed. It read 'Garner Wilde'. No wonder the private detective Wilde's son had hired was able to track me down.

There was another entry on my birth record that was a lot more surprising than seeing 'Garner Wilde' in the 'Father's Name' box. It was seeing 'May 1' in the 'Date of Birth' box. I was four days closer to fifty than I realized!

I removed my alarm clock from my backpack and set it for 7:00 am. I slept on the floor behind the counter. After the alarm went off, I relocated to the bathroom, both to use it and to hide until Maddus came to work, unlocked the door, and eventually went to the back for some reason. At which point, I left.

I was thankful for two things about the

records office. First, the heat was not turned off at night. It was not so cold that I would have frozen, but I would have had trouble sleeping.

The second feature was the lack of a motion sensor or other alarm devices. I wasn't surprised that laid-back Silver City had not bothered to protect the records office. It's not a bank or a jewelry store. Nothing valuable to protect.

Except the truth.

I had no fear that my illegal activity would be discovered. I had left only one clue that I was back among the files. Not fingerprints; I wore gloves. No picture to be identified by facial recognition software. There were no cameras. But I did leave some DNA because holding the penlight in my mouth caused me to drool on the files.

Before heading to Albuquerque, I drove past Silver City High School up to an area on the north edge of town called Dos Griegos where there are houses scattered around the hills on big lots. And many vacant lots waiting to be sold. I found a big open lot on a street called Aleco Way. It seemed like an Omen. *Alecko* is a Greek name meaning `protector of the people`.

I hiked up to Gomez Peak where I had a good view of the area occupied by the ancient Mimbres people. Evidently, they didn't have a protector. They vanished from the earth a thousand years ago, but they are still remembered and admired for their pottery. I buried the pot shard at the top of the mountain.

Chapter 34

I told Sharice I'd found what I'd expected. My parents had agreed to adopt me and hire my birth mother as a nanny so that she would be able to help raise her own son, and they would have a child.

She said, "It worked perfectly."

"Yes. It did. I'm lucky to have had three parents. The only sad part is I had a brother I didn't know about. I think I would have liked him."

"Why?"

"He followed his father's wish that they try to find me even though it would reduce his inheritance. They found a Mimbres pottery shard in his pocket. I think he was bringing it to me as a sort of symbol of the place where his father fathered me. And he liked to read."

I looked at Sharice. "You would have liked him, too. He wore designer clothes."

She laughed.

"In addition to verifying what I thought I'd figured out about my birth, I also found a small surprise."

"A pleasant one?"

"No, but not unpleasant. Just confusing. For my whole life, I've been celebrating my birthday on the wrong date."

"You weren't born on May 5th?"

"Nope. May 1st. Says so on the birth record. Weird, right?"

She thought for a few seconds then said, "I think I can explain it. I think your parents wanted some token of your ethnic heritage, so they chose *Cinco de Mayo* as your birth date, a little secret they shared with Consuela their entire lives. And since the records were sealed, they figured no one would ever know."

"I think you're right. So now the only thing that confuses me is that I was rejected as a donor when Consuela needed a kidney transplant. How can that be if she and I share DNA?"

She said, "Kidney transplant donors and recipients don't have to have any DNA relation. They just need to have compatible blood types. A mother and her child often have different blood types. So that must have been the case."

Good to have a health care worker as a girlfriend. Make that fiancé.

She paused a moment then asked, "Does Consuela know that you know?"

"I'm sure she doesn't."

"Will you tell her?"

"No."

She nodded. "I think that's the right thing. She's happy knowing her son is getting married and she's finally going to have a grandchild, although no one will know it's hers. So now what?"

"We get married. We have a child. Maybe more than one. We live happily ever after."

"What about the inheritance? You can't very well tell Ninfa she's your half-sister and therefore gets part of Garner Wilde's estate."

I shrugged. "I've been paying for her parents' health care all these years under false pretenses. If I get the inheritance, I'll figure out some way to give her a portion without turning her life upside down."

"What about *your* life being turned upside down?"

"It felt like that at first. Now it doesn't. My parents are still the people who raised me. They were assisted by a nanny, who was in fact my biological mother. I've always loved all three of them. Still do. The biology is different from what I thought, but people aren't their biology. Nor are they their gender or their ethnicity. People are their personality, each one a unique combination of values, desires, talents, fears, faults, insights and dreams. It's reflected in our countenance. Not in our DNA. My parents and my nanny are the same now as they were then. And now I'll have a child of my own, and I'll try to raise her the way my parents and nanny raised me."

She laughed. "You're sticking with that

theory that we'll have a girl because we have sex frequently."

"Frequently is good."

"It is," she said and kissed me.

Author's Postscript

When readers ask if Hubie is based on me, I usually answer that part of him comes from an amalgam of people from my past and part comes purely from my imagination.

But there is something Hubie and I have in common. We were both adopted.

When I started the series, I didn't know Hubie was adopted. I wanted him to be a bit eccentric, so I gave him older parents who would not put him in little league baseball but would buy him books. I gave him a nanny. I had no idea she would turn out to be his mother.

I know only two things about my own birth mother – she was unmarried, and she decided to put me up for adoption, for which I am eternally grateful.

Abortion was illegal in Texas when I was conceived, but my birth mother may have been able to find someone to provide that service. Had she chosen to do so, I would never have existed, an abstract counterfactual that doesn't deserve much attention.

My real mother – Billie Louise Grisham Orenduff, the woman who raised me – was a wonderful, nurturing woman. My real father – Jess Johnson Orenduff, the man who raised me – was a terrific father.

By coincidence, my father and I were both

tall. People who met us would often remark that we looked alike. In fact, we did not look much alike. But because he was my father, I probably adopted many of his mannerisms. So we were alike in ways that belied our lack of shared genes. Better than genes, we shared countenances.

My real parents handled the adoption issue perfectly. They told me I was adopted in such a way that it sounded like a trivial detail, like being chubby or liking beans. And they told me so early that I can't remember not knowing it. I have known I'm adopted for my entire life, just as you have known your name for your entire life.

Over the years, people have asked me if I've ever tried to find out more about my "real" parents. I answer that my real parents are the ones who raised me.

Two years after I was adopted, my parents gave birth to a daughter. As Pat and I grew up, I often reminded her that our parents *chose* me but had to take her no matter what. Pat is not biologically related to me, but there is no doubt that she is my real sister.

Acknowledgements

Because this book has a peculiar history, writing the acknowledgements was almost more difficult than writing the story.

After finishing the first draft of the book in the summer of 2019, the next step was to send copies to my stalwart beta-readers. The group changes a bit with each book. A few volunteers are added. Sometimes an author friend declines because he or she is in the middle of a project. A few beta readers have passed.

As I was thinking about it, I remembered that the Left Coast Crime convention was scheduled for March in San Diego, and I was on the program to give a presentation - "How to become a best-selling author," done partially in fun but with real advice about doing so. And I remembered that LCC gives each attendee a bag of goodies – pens, stickers, notepads, coffee mugs, etc. But mostly books. So I decided to send enough rough copies of the book so that every attendee would get one. And right after the title page, I added an author's note inviting everyone to send me suggestions and comments.

I arrived in San Diego the night before the conference was to begin and registered the next morning. The first day had a limited number of events and a presentation that evening. That was when I found out that the conference had been ordered to shut down because the county health department was banning all large gatherings because of the corona virus.

After I got home, I had a flood of emails from people who had read the draft. I even had some who sent me their copy with marks in the margins and/or corrections scribbled into the text. I received text messages on my cell phone, voice mails, and some regular phone calls. And I did a poor job of keeping track of it all.

So first, I want to acknowledge and thank all of those who gave me feedback. And second, I want to apologize to anyone I fail to mention and/or fail to credit with the right suggestion. I used almost all the suggestions you made. I tried to correct all the typos and errors you found. The book is better for your efforts even if I confuse who made what effort. What follows is my imperfect list of acknowledgementees. Is that a word?

Thanks first to Bruce Williams who put in almost as much work on this book as I did. He found many typos, made dozens of helpful suggestions, and asked a bunch of astute questions that led me to make changes.

Thanks to Sharon Snyder of the Los Alamos Historical Museum for fact-checking that Edith Warner did not have a son as was alleged in an interview in the Voices of the Manhattan Project, and for other bits of information about Warner.

Thanks to Dave Cordova of Taos for finding 10 typos that I had missed even though I'd read the thing several hundred time. I knew Dave was smart, but I didn't realize he has an editor's eye.

Thanks to Paul and Laura Bates for finding a huge time sequence flaw and for numerous other excellent suggestions. Their knowledge of the series (and the fact that they both seem to have excellent recall) helped me get this latest book better synchronize with the first eight.

Thanks to Betsy Cornwell for pointing out that Hubie would prefer his Gruet in a flute rather than a coupe. But he wisely defers to Sharice's preference for the coupes.

Thanks to Linda McNab for suggesting a change in the scene where Bette Wilde shoots the Hawaiian sling at Hubie that made it clear why it did not injure or kill him.

Thanks to Bob Hammon for pointing out that the story would have more of a New Mexico feel if the weapon had been an atlatl dipped in Gila monster venom rather than a Hawaiian sling! I like the idea but couldn't face the total re-write it would have required.

Thanks to Karen Ballard for assistance with the list of New Mexico mystery writers.

Thanks to Lisa Davis whom I have known since I was in the third grade. She helped me correct several awkward passages.

Thanks to Robert Maynard who suggested a re-write of the part where the door on Jollo Bakkie's door is changed. Robert is an architect, so it was nice to have professional help, and he didn't even charge me. He also found a number of typos.

Thanks to Susan Smith who caught a weird phrase – muddy from play – which the context suggested should have been muddy with clay. Turns out no change was needed, but I did have to check it.

Thanks to anthropologist/archaeologist Tom Lake who fact-checks all my books and also makes great suggestions.

Thanks to Susan Braun, a great editor and an even greater friend.

Finally, thanks to the woman whose name I have forgotten and whose card I have misplaced who got a copy of the ARC at Treasure House Books and Gifts in Old Town, Albuquerque and sent it back to me with about a hundred sticky notes and inserted helpful suggested changes. If you read this and contact me, I'll add your name in the next printing.

The same goes for anyone else I have omitted. It has been terrific to be part of such a large team, and I want to acknowledge you all.

The Pot Thief books in order of publication

1. The Pot Thief who Studied Pythagoras

2. The Pot Thief who Studied Ptolemy

3. The Pot Thief who Studied Einstein

4. The Pot Thief who Studied Escoffier

5. The Pot Thief who Studied D. H. Lawrence

6. The Pot Thief who Studied Billy the Kid

7. The Pot Thief who Studied Georgia O'Keeffe

8. The Pot Thief who Studied Edward Abbey

9. The Pot Thief who Studied the Woman at Otowi Crossing

10. The Pot Thief who Studied ______?______

Suggestions welcome. ThePotThief@gmail.com

CPSIA information can be obtained
at www.ICGtesting.com
Printed in the USA
LVHW111444250920
667115LV00001B/62